Princess of Undersea

Endless Press
15 S Church St
Spring City, PA 19475
Info@EndlessPress.org
www.EndlessPress.org

ISBN 978-0-9862250-6-2

This book is dedicated to my parents, who did their part to instill in me a love of stories and filled our home with quality books that taught me the timeless nature of literature and the value of creating a story that will still be read and cherished by future generations for centuries to come.

Princess of Undersea

by Leslie Conzatti

Endless Press

EndlessPress.org

Contents

Chapter 1

Undersea and Overcliff

Deep below the murky green of the Shallow Waters, far beyond the resilience of any diver lay the spires of Undersea. It is a place no living man has seen, for one must surely drown and sink beyond any method of rescue in order to penetrate the upper reaches of the kingdom.

The great coral palace, with its rosy formations, towered over the rest of the city. Round spheres formed the various rooms, each with one main opening large enough for a full-grown Merman to swim through, and several smaller ones to let in the sunlight. In the largest of these, King Davor of the Mer-people swam back and forth in agitation.

His daughter, Ylaine, was missing. Not that he had no idea where she was—there were only a few places she could be, and out of those, Davor was certain he knew which one she might choose. The question was:

why? What had he done to deserve an offspring who did not do and stay as she was told? Did she not realize that these boundaries were for her safety? Davor paused to regard his reflection on the surface of a highly-polished obsidian crystal. His grey skin complimented his wavy, dark hair. The King's Medallion—a sea biscuit shaped of solid gold—hung about his neck. Just the sight of it inspired reverence in all Merfolk—all except one.

Did Ylaine not care that he was king?

"Your highness! We have found the Princess!"

King Davor turned as two Mer-guards entered the chamber.

"Well?" He prompted, his amber eyes flashing. "Where is she?"

The second guard flexed his tail up behind him and stretched his arms toward it, bending his head forward in a gesture of respect. "My liege, Princess Ylaine requested that we escort her to her royal chambers."

"Her royal chambers?" Davor was so furious, his tail went as stiff as a pike's. "The Royal Undersea Convention is gathering, and my daughter thinks she can just go to her room?"

Neither guard met his gaze; they were too busy bowing Mer-fashion. With a twist of his tail, the irate king exploded out of the chamber's opening and toward a round coral colony on the other side of the palace.

Ylaine drifted with the current in the middle of the space. Her violet hair hung in a tangled cloud around her face.

Davor paused to cool his fury before entering.

"Ylaine?" He called softly.

"I am here, Father," she answered as he swam inside.

"My dear, are you ready for the convening of the Council?"

Ylaine sighed and swam forward, letting the water pressure carry her tresses aside to expose her blue-skinned face. She turned her mournful aquamarine eyes upon her father. "Not today, please, Father. I do not feel well."

Davor's throat-gills snapped impatiently. "Ylaine, please; just once, that's all I ask."

Ylaine snapped her gills too, though considerably a smaller noise than her father made. "That is just what you've said every time, Father."

"Ylaine," Davor continued evenly, "You know I like to hear you sing."

Ylaine pressed her lips in a smile. "Then why don't you listen, Father?"

"Such a gift as yours is only fitting for an event like this one."

"I am quite sure the fairy did not give it to me to be used in such a manner."

"Please, Ylaine—"

"I told you," Ylaine twisted so her hair concealed her face again. "I'm not well. I need to rest."

Davor folded his muscled arms across his smooth torso. "This wouldn't have anything to do with the fact that I'm sure the guards found you trying to slip through the boundaries in a school of barracuda, would it?"

A single flicker of the aqua eye among the purple haze confirmed his suspicion.

"I just wanted to see the surface, just once!" she complained.

"Ylaine, you know that this cannot be—"

"Oh yes, because humans are careless and cruel and they'd as soon chop off my tail as look at me!"

"Ylaine!"

"Nayidia says that it used to be a tradition for all Merfolk who so desire to swim to the surface at the Great Moon Rising." She babbled without looking at him. "Nearly three hundred Great Moons have passed, and never have I seen another Mermaid pass your precious boundary! We have delved deeper into the seabed, when we might be rising up, and on!"

"Enough!" Davor ordered. "You know those boundaries are placed there for your protection."

"Protection from what?" Ylaine demanded. "You know me, Father; I would never willfully place myself in danger. You have taught me to pay attention to my surroundings—"

"It is the humans, Ylaine," Davor began.

Ylaine twisted away from him and began swimming around the room, picking ropes of seaweed and placing them in her hair. "Oh yes, father," she grumbled. "Tell me again how evil the humans are, how dangerous are their crafts in which they sit, waiting for the odd flash of fish-scales to strike with their harpoons. You know," she stopped and confronted her father as her hair splayed out around her face, "I am sure the human world has changed since the fairies left—"

Davor frowned. "What would you know about that? There have been only rumors for years!"

"Nayidia told me about them. The old days are not such a secret thing. I bet if you went up and saw for yourself, no harm would come to you, and you'd call off this wretched vendetta you have created for yourself!" She sat before the obsidian mirror and turned her back to her father.

"Please, Ylaine." Davor placed his hands over his daughter's shoulders and plucked a white starfish from the obsidian, then folded his daughter's hair back from her face and fastened it there with the star. Still, she kept her eyes down. He tipped her chin up.

"You're beautiful and I love you," he murmured.

Finally, Ylaine met his gaze. "Love me, and conduct the Council using your own words to convince the Merfolk that your plan is worthwhile."

"You know how the Councilors are; nothing I say will sway them. They do not heed my warnings, claiming that a war against an unconfirmed enemy is not just."

"Why, have you not sent scouts beyond the boundary?" Ylaine turned to glare at him again. "What makes you so certain that this war is truly what you want?"

"The humans must be stopped," said Davor, handing his daughter a rope of seaweed with which to tie her hair.

Reluctantly, Ylaine accepted it and began binding her wild tresses into a long braid that hung behind her head. This she wound around itself in a large knot, which she held in place with another sea star. She paused to evaluate the effect in the smooth rock-face, staring at her father's reflection pointedly.

"What are they doing, that they must cease? Are their divers reaching lower and lower depths? What happened to trading with them, as in the ancient days?"

Davor hesitated; it is true, there was once a time when Fairies and Merfolk traded freely with the humans, surfacing regularly to barter rare and fascinating items from the seabed.

"Those days are over," Davor said slowly. "Remember what happened to your mother?"

"Only what you have told me, Not even Nayidia dares to explain more." Ylaine replied quietly, giving her father a mournful glance. "But Father," she rejoined in earnest, "that was one boat, that was one time—"

"I have lost one love," Davor said, embracing his daughter. "I will not lose another. I love you, My Princess." He held her for a moment, and nodded to the guard that respectfully appeared at the entrance overhead.

"It is time," he said, pulling away and looking at his daughter. She was growing more and more beautiful every day. King Davor made his request one last time.

"Will you do this for me, Daughter? For your mother?"

Ylaine sighed, her gills popping in her throat as they flexed. "Very well, Father."

Davor nodded and handed her the golden cowrie shell that marked her as royalty. "Your mother would be proud to see the gift she witnessed put to such a noble use," he told her.

Behind his back, Ylaine felt the shell bounce against her neck as she muttered, "No, she wouldn't father. Not this… not at all."

✧✧✧

In the Great Hall, dignitaries from all four corners of the Sea gathered to meet with King Davor of Undersea. They straightened out of respect when the Princess entered. The King came in behind her.

"Merpeople of the Sea!" he greeted them. "My daughter, the Princess Ylaine, you know is the most wonderful

Voice of the Ocean. A wise fairy blessed her with the gift of song when she was born. I have asked that she sing for you now, as a special welcome to Undersea." He nudged the reluctant girl. "Go ahead."

Ylaine cleared the frown from her face as she drew herself up to her full length, all seven feet. She tilted her head back as light from the sun shone down through a gap in the coral walls of the palace and illuminated her figure. She opened her mouth and began to sing. The haunting melody captivated her audience. The tones rolling from her mouth did more than excite their ears; the magic of her voice resonated deep within those who heard it. The piercing notes subtly danced along the streams of their consciousness, pulling them into a new configuration, one more open and receptive to the impending message. When she finished, they remained with their eyes glued to her, mesmerized by her song. Davor nodded and she left as he came into the beam of sunlight. Now all attention was focused on him.

"Men of the Sea," he cried, "are you ready to hear me?"

As one, they answered him, "We will listen to what you have to say."

Davor smiled, "Then let the Royal Council begin."

✦✦✦

High up on the top of the stone cliffs that formed the boundary for Undersea stood the royal palace of the island kingdom of Overcliff.

Within the palace, a dark-haired young man with sharp features crouched in the shadows, curled up as small as his lanky frame would allow. He waited, counting silently to himself.

"Five… four… three… two… *one!*" He slipped out just as the guards were changing. Hugging the wall and keeping well below any windows, the grey-clad young man crept toward his goal. One more corner, one more hallway—

At last! The mischievous rogue squeezed into an alcove and surveyed his quarry: a fresh berry tart on the windowsill. He would have to slip past the pastry chef, the cook, the cellar-maid, the baker, and the footmen traipsing in and out of the kitchen as they readied luncheon for His Majesty—

"Your Highness!" The cry hurt his pride almost as much as the fierce grip hurt his ear.

"Aww, Giles!" he whined, gripping the servant's wrist in a vain attempt at getting him to relax his grip.

Giles never relented. "Prince Nathan, what do you think you're doing?" His eyes immediately went for the tart. "Devising plans of insubordination, I see. And tell me, Prince—would it really have tasted as sweet to gulp it down in the last few minutes before luncheon so that you would not get caught, or to wait until you had finished your meal, at which time you would be able to call for it and consume at your leisure?" Giles laughed and hauled the prince ignominiously out to the hallway. Only then did he release him.

"Ow, Giles," Nathan rubbed his tender lobe. "I could have you whipped for that, you know."

"I am fulfilling the duties laid down by your father of looking after you, Prince," Giles replied soberly. He snorted, "Besides, if you whipped everyone who dared speak against you, what sort of king would that make you?"

"One with less bruises, that is certain," Nathan muttered. "Now go and fetch my boots!"

Giles glanced at his stocking feet and shook his head. "Ah, nay, My Prince. You and I both will return to your chambers. It would not do to stuff those sorry, dusty scraps into your nice clean boots that I've just shined, now would it?"

Nathan groaned and followed Giles back to his room.

༄༅

In the Great Hall, King Theodore pored over the sheaf of documents his advisors had delivered to his desk. A blanket of melancholy settled over his brain and fairly muddled the propositions for new taxes and laws, the reports on the royal treasury, and the state of the kingdom. Pushing them aside, he picked up the map that outlined the various farms in Overcliff, and the amount of fertile ground used for planting, with small sections in each farm set aside for the royal storehouses. Theodore pulled at his thinning grey beard as his sagging, wrinkled forehead creased in bewildered concern. He would have to get the Royal Archivist to bring him the last map of such kind, but he could have sworn the areas left for the farmers and their families grew smaller and smaller each year, as did the merchandise reports from the marketplace. Meanwhile, the census seemed to increase for a few years, and then drop sharply—where did people go, anymore? King Theodore set aside his papers and rubbed his aching head. He could tighten his belt to one-course meals during the day—but what about Nathan? The Prince was a growing boy, and he ought to have all the sustenance he required.

He returned to the petition from his advisors. They had taken to sending petitions written up on paper and borne by messenger, ever since the last actual convening of the court had ended in disaster.

"The coffers are low," one councilor had complained. "And Overcliff has little hope of ever recovering from the last bad harvest. Trade has suffered since the banishment of the fairies, Milord; perhaps we might consider rescinding the order?"

King Theodore's face had hardened at the idea.

"Such a move would be disastrous!" protested the fat man sitting next to him. "After all, weren't the fairies responsible for bringing the plague that killed so many humans—including the Queen, may angels bless her soul?"

The king's chin trembled and he covered his mouth as the memory of his beloved wife washed over him yet again. Queen Theresa, with her shining smile and those star-like eyes she passed on to her son! King Theodore had never been stronger than with his beloved wife at his side, whispering her wise words in his ear when the shouting advisors would poison his mind with their suggestions of taxation and reaping the best from the people merely because he was king and the commoners could not gainsay the king's word.

"Baeram, we've been over this," sighed another. "The fairies had all pulled back to the mainland before anyone could find proof that it was the fairies who brought it."

Baeram waved his arms. "How else do you explain the fact that no cure could even touch it—not even the inhuman arts of the fairies themselves? People died, Cassar! What more proof do you need?" He wagged his head as the other councilors took the king's distant silence as tacit permission to murmur in his presence.

"No, the embargo stands. Our only recourse is taxation—or an alliance with another kingdom." His eyes slid over to King Theodore. "The young prince is of age, but that is not to say we have lost the opportunity for His Majesty to take another queen—"

The king's gaze finally returned to the matter. The talk of finances and complaints about the embargo had always swirled around his head—now they would presume to sully the memory of his beloved Theresa?

"Enough!" He barked, his whole body trembling.

All sound died as the councilors stared at him.

"She is my Queen!" He rasped. "My Queen, and the fairies would have nothing to do with her! Therefore we have nothing to do with fairies! Get your petty treason out of my chambers!"

The meeting had ended there; the indolent councilors departed the chamber as fast as their plump and doddering legs could carry them. Theodore had lapsed back into passive introspection as the poorly-framed proposals of the men he depended on to aid him in running the country had instead dredged up painful memories.

Now, viewing the same old petitions meticulously worded and heavy with technicalities, the king shook his head, still as resolute on the issue as ever. Welcome the fairies back? After what they had done to incur their banishment? By no means! Trade with the fairies had benefited the kingdom, surely, but since that black day more than twenty years ago, King Theodore was faced in his advancing age with the prospect of leading the kingdom alone, with no one to speak boldly in his support. He had entrusted the tutelage of his young son to a worthy servant named Giles, in the hopes that young Nathan would eventually grow as wise as his mother had been—but that day had not come yet. Still, King Theodore hoped.

The great bell sounded, announcing that all was in readiness for the midday meal. King Theodore smiled and pushed aside his papers as Prince Nathan came into the room, booted, laughing, and fairly exuding life and vitality. Close on his heels followed his faithful steward, Giles.

"Ah, my son!" Theodore gushed, as Nathan took his seat at the right-hand corner of the table nearest his father. The foot-servants entered, placing several dishes before the prince, and a few before the king.

Nathan didn't seem to notice, and dug into the repast with a relish.

"Have you had a good day today, Nathan?" King Theodore asked, picking slowly over his simple meal of roasted meat and vegetables.

Nathan paused in his consumption of an entire roast hen and shrugged. "Well enough, if Giles would not insist on dragging me off to practice sparring or learn geogramy and tripe like that. But I was able to catch Tom this morning on his way to university." Nathan grabbed a handful of grapes from the platter in front of him and began decimating the cluster, still talking all the while. "I think we're going to go hunting once he finishes his studies this afternoon."

Theodore nodded, grinning at his energetic son. "A worthy pastime, indeed!" he said. "I am sure Giles will be of great assistance; perhaps you may bag your dinner!"

"Giles?" Nathan glanced at his silent steward and shrugged. "No, I don't think I'd want him around. He might make me chart the circumberance of the forest or something boring like that. If it's all the same, I think Tom will do just fine."

"What about the village boy in your patronage? What was his name?"

Nathan paused and considered very hard. "Oh yes, the chap I'm sponsoring with that Royal scholarship at the University? Whatsisname, Paul? Peter? Hmph, I cannot remember! Giles, do you know?"

Giles kept his expression neutral as he replied, "I believe the young lad's name was Simon, your Highness."

"That's it, Simon! How old must he be now, you think?"

"If I recall, Highness, he is but five years your junior."

"You don't say!" Nathan fiddled with the bones on his plate as he mulled over the plan. "I suppose if I'm paying for his education, I might as well invite Simon along on the hunting trip, wouldn't it, Father?"

"Of course," said King Theodore. "A king ought to be a man who is willing to associate with his people. Go to, my son!"

"Thanks, father!" Nathan sprang up from the table to receive his friend Tom and send for the boy Simon.

Theodore laid down his napkin and moved away from the table to allow the servants to clear the dishes. Giles remained where he was until Theodore beckoned him to join him at the window.

"I worry about him, Giles," said Theodore heavily. "I am nearing the end of my reign, and he seems to have no interest in kingly things."

"Aye, Milord," agreed Giles, "if it was a lady distracting him that would be one thing, but Nathan's diversion seems to center on himself."

Theodore's face folded on itself as he pondered this. He wagged his head. "No, I do not think romance is necessary for a King. I do wish he would show a little more interest in matters of the kingdom." He chuckled. "My mind is not as spry as it once was, and yet my duties do not get any simpler."

The steward pressed his lips. "If I may speak freely, Sire," he began slowly.

Theodore nodded, watching his son ride out of the courtyard flanked by his friends. "I will hear it, Giles. I always have."

Giles chose his words carefully. "If you were to invite your son to these council meetings, or to assign him some small part of kingly duties, just to give him some impression of what will be expected of him—"

Theodore turned away from the window and began pacing back to the pile of documents at the table. "No, no; I am old, yes, but Nathan is still young—what, only just past a score, is he?"

"A score and five, my lord."

"Ah me! Time is a sprightly dame, is she not? But, be that as it may, I think the Prince shall have time enough to settle down; these things can wait till he has the mind for them. If there is one thing I have learned, Giles, it is that one's family is more valuable than one's rank. Let the boy have his play. He'll be a man soon enough."

Chapter 2

The Wish

Ylaine left a trail of silvery bubbles as she sped through the water, her smooth, narrow body perfectly aligned with her tail extended straight behind her like a shining, black harpoon. Let them talk! Until Davor could figure out how to enable the Merfolk to breathe out of the water, the human kingdom was far enough away from the shore to be safe. Ylaine swam out to the open water. She could see the King's Boundary from here: a thin, silver shimmer barely visible, but watched keenly at every moment, along every inch by rotating squads of soldiers.

"It might as well have been a net!" Ylaine huffed, yanking out the seaweed ropes so that her hair floated outward, free of its restraints. She swam downward, toward the shadowy cave system below the mainland side.

A massive ship lay embedded in the sand and coral down there—half of it, anyway. The stern of a large warship lay among the rock, crusted with barnacles and home to all sorts of shallow life that enjoyed the soft wood as an alternative to impenetrable stone. Ylaine swam over to the mast. Placing her hands around the top, she traced lazy patterns in the algae as she drifted in circles all the way down to the deck. There were only a few casks and chests left with anything in them. There had been divers who tried to recover the cargo, long before Ylaine was born, but the wreck was too deep—and besides, there were the sharks. They circled the deck as Ylaine watched, big, stupid, grey things that paid no attention to anything that wasn't swimming right in front of them and small enough to eat. They seemed to find humans delectable enough. Ylaine let her fingers trail over the back of a passing nurse shark as she wondered if perhaps it was because human blood carried a stronger scent in the water than that of any other animal. A tiger shark swam over her, and Ylaine giggled; with the markings on its back and head, it almost looked exactly like her father!

"Now there's music I would know anywhere!" Cried a voice from the depths of the hull. With a flip of her tail, Ylaine twisted around and swam down to what used to be the captain's quarters.

An older Merwoman sat upon the tarnished brass bed frame. Her deep-blue tail spread out before her, as she wound her dark-red braids around her like long, thick sashes.

"Hello Nayidia!" said Ylaine, drawing near to the Mermaid with skin so pale-blue it was almost white. Nayidia had served as Ylaine's nurse after the disappearance of her mother, and later on accepted the role of godmother to the young Merprincess. Ylaine made no secret of the fact that she regarded Nayidia as the mother-figure she never had.

Nayidia's blue eyes gleamed as she smiled. "Ylaine, my little Kelpling! Do you know, you crossed my mind several times this morning as I was out searching the shipyards."

Ylaine relished the thrill that ran from her shoulders to the tip of her tail whenever Nayidia mentioned the shipyards: a vast underwater valley just beyond the Boundary filled with the wrecks of warships, cruise ships and merchant ships that had all been lost to the humans over the ages.

"Ooh!" She gushed, "What did you find this time?"

Nayidia smiled and gestured to a trunk in the corner. "Open that, my dear. I found many things to show you."

Ylaine swam over to the chest in question. Nayidia was always finding fascinating trinkets that once belonged to humans among the wrecks, and by far Ylaine was the only Mermaid at all interested in the stuff.

On the top of the pile was a small human made of a hard material Ylaine assumed was coral, with some kind of frilly covering wrapped around it. Ylaine explored the stiff limbs of the creature.

"Oh, how beautiful!" She gasped.

Nayidia smiled. "You like the doll? Humans like to build prettier, miniature versions of themselves."

Ylaine looked closely at the lower appendages. Though there were two, she noticed something odd. "Nayidia, don't the humans have little fingers on the bottom ones?" She pointed to the solid flipper-like appendages of the doll.

"Toes, you mean? Toes on the feet? Yes, they do." Nayidia was nearly the last of the generation who traded with humans, so she was the one Mermaid in Ylaine's life who could discuss them. "The dolls don't have them because the dolls cannot move by themselves, and besides, the feet are always closed up in boots, so why shape them?"

So many new words soon bewildered the Merprincess, so she set down the doll and moved on.

"What is this?" She pulled out something round and smooth and flat.

"That's a plate, dear."

"What's this?" Ylaine pulled out a huge mass of the sort of covering the doll had.

"Oh, that?" Nayidia laughed as Ylaine let the thing

float by itself in the water. "It's called a dress. Humans wear clothes all the time."

"They do?" Ylaine swam under the thing and slipped her lithe body inside. She felt as large and ungainly as a sea cow, and every movement she tried was stifled by the waterlogged fabric. Both Mermaids laughed at the comical nature of the human fashion.

"Humph! Maybe they wear these things to keep from flying away!" Ylaine concluded, swimming out again. She spotted a painting with a long green fishtail and pulled out the dish. What she saw confused her: the creature depicted looked more like a human with a fishtail attached—not at all like the Merfolk of Undersea. Ylaine showed the plate to her godmother.

"Look, Nayidia!" she giggled. "Humans with fishtails!"

Nayidia gave a smirk as she took the plate and shook her head. "Not quite; I believe this is what human artists think a mermaid looks like."

Ylaine gave a confused wriggle. "Really? But where are the gills? Why does she have those lumpy things?" Ylaine blew a stream of small, mocking bubbles. Even the doll's smooth belly was more accurate to her own flat torso than this parody.

Nayidia curled her scaly body into a circle. "That human half is actually what most female humans look like on top—just with legs instead of a tail. This is, unfortunately, their standard of beauty, on the surface.

They have no idea how difficult it would actually be to survive in the water with skin—" she pointed to the pale human part, "instead of scales," and then to the fishtail.

"Especially a mermaid with so much skin as that," Ylaine chuckled at the corpulent figure as she tried to see if her chest would puff out in the same way. It did not, and she resumed pulling things out of the trunk.

"Oh, oh! I know what these are!" Excited, Ylaine pulled a handful of pearl and diamond necklaces out of the trunk. She hung them around her neck and floated before the obsidian mirror to admire herself.

"Yes, just yesterday I found what must have been a royal cruise ship, because there were hundreds of treasures on board. You would not believe the riches beyond the reach of humans down there!"

Ylaine rattled her throat gills enviously. "Oh, I wish I could go with you!" Her eyes pleaded with Nayidia.

The older Mermaid shook her head. "You know your father has forbidden everyone else from going out there."

"But you do it!"

"Kelpling," Nayidia returned wryly, "I am old. I'm not the one trying to go to the surface all the time. If I die, it is Fate. You are the Crown Princess," she pointed to the cowrie shell among the pearls and gems. "And your father gave the order. You should do as he says. Maybe he'll change his mind someday."

"He'll never change his mind!" Ylaine exploded.

Nayidia frowned sympathetically. She held out her hands to Ylaine. "Come here." She picked up an implement that was dark, shiny, and prickly.

"What's that?" asked Ylaine.

"This is a comb. Humans use that to make their hair smooth and shiny. Want me to show you?" Nayidia emphasized her point by attempting to suppress Ylaine's constant cloud of violet hair.

Ylaine shrugged and settled down in front of her nurse. "I suppose."

Nayidia began at the very ends of Ylaine's hair, combing the teeth through the strands.

"Did you have a bad day?" She asked.

Ylaine's throat-gills rattled as she sighed and came to rest upon the frame beside her onetime nurse. "Kind of," she said, as her hair crept forward on the current to hide her face. "Father made me sing before the council again."

Nayidia drew the comb with long soothing strokes through Ylaine's hair. "Oh I'm sure it was beautiful."

Ylaine popped her gills. "Don't ask him; he always stops his ears." She pursed her lips. "Why does he do that? I mean, I know it's a fairy gift, but why do Merfolk act strangely whenever I sing?"

"Did your father ever tell you just what the fairy said when she blessed you?" Nayidia asked carefully.

"He probably wasn't listening; he never listens," Ylaine complained.

"I remember your mother, Queen Yssandra, cradling you in her arms as the fairy spoke the words. Her blessing was thus: *May the music of your voice bring comfort to the heavy heart, courage to the fearful heart, wisdom to the foolish one, and truth to the hearts darkened by falsehood. May those whose hearts are noble be drawn by the sound of your gift.*"

"Wisdom to the foolish heart?" Ylaine repeated with scorn. "I wish I could sing to my father, then; his heart's as foolish as the minds of the other leaders."

"You did sing for him once, long ago," Nayidia replied quietly. "The day your mother died. You sang and soothed his grief." The comb came up as far as Ylaine's scalp.

The Merprincess spoke slowly. "And he hasn't listened since." She stopped and turned to look at the older Mermaid.

Nayidia gently guided Ylaine's head back to facing forward. "Yes, and more's the pity. You know, sometimes I can't help thinking that—well, meaning no disrespect to the King, of course…"

Ylaine felt her whole body relax into the soothing strokes of the comb. "What do you think, Nayidia?"

The Merwoman paused to untangle a knot of violet hair. "Well, ever since your dear mother vanished, I can't help noticing that—I think perhaps your father might be afraid, dear."

Ylaine twisted to face her, even as she still combed out the ends of her hair. "Why?" she asked. "Does he fear me? Is my gift dangerous?" Alarm flashed in the aquamarine eyes.

Naiyidia smiled reassuringly. "We all fear things we do not understand, but that fear doesn't make them dangerous." She put her hand on Ylaine's shoulder and gave a little push. "Turn around, Kelpling. I'm not finished."

Ylaine obeyed, settling down for more combing as she considered her godmother's words. "So Father thinks I would harm him if he listens to me?"

"Perhaps he is worried that if you sing and make him forget his grief, he would forget about your mother entirely."

Again, Ylaine whirled around in fright. "I would never do that to him!"

Nayidia stopped combing and looked into her god-daughter's eyes. "But you might; think about it—he controls when and how you use the gift every time, but you and I both know that this is not how a powerful gift like yours ought to be used. Who knows what you might be capable of if you were allowed to use it properly?"

Ylaine turned back around as Nayidia began braiding her hair. She pondered what her godmother said;

certainly she had harbored the very same sentiments that morning. Perhaps her father was afraid; but then how could she rescue him from that fear?

"Why does he make you sing before every council?" she asked patiently.

Ylaine stroked the soft body of an anemone clinging to the bed frame. "Because he wants to lead a war against the humans," she answered, "and he needs everyone to do as he says in order to accomplish it."

Nayidia considered this. "And you think he makes you sing just because it is easier than having to justify himself."

Ylaine flicked her tail. "Of course! I almost wonder," she mused as she twiddled the comb in her hands, "if my gift is more of a curse than a blessing—but at the same time, I cannot imagine life without it."

Nayidia finished braiding Ylaine's hair and fastened it not with seaweed but with a silk ribbon like what humans used.

"I could show you," she said quickly.

Ylaine turned to face her. "What do you mean?"

Nayidia patiently hovered in front of Ylaine, looking deep into her eyes as she asked, "What would you say if I told you I knew of a water-fairy who had a spell that could temporarily remove a fairy-gift?"

Ylaine gasped and her eyes sparkled. "A water-fairy? I thought fairies only flew in the sky!"

Nayidia smiled and swam around animatedly, gesturing with her hands. "Oh no, Kelpling! You see, many generations ago, all the elements had Fae who could manipulate them. There were water-fairies who swam in the water as we do, and earth-fairies who scampered along the ground, sky-fairies who made their homes in the clouds—all of them! These were the ones to visit us during the Great Moon Rising—"

Ylaine clapped her hands to her face with glee. "Oh!" She gave a little wriggle to settle deeper into her spot. "Does this mean you're going to tell me the story of the First Great Moon Rising, Godmother?"

Nayidia laughed, the sound rippling over her gills like the bubbles out of her mouth. "You silly little angelfish! Why, I must have told you the story at least twice before."

"I know," Ylaine said quickly, carving a few more twirls in the water and admiring the movement of her new braid—just like Nayidia's. "But I just love it so much! Hearing you talk about it is the closest I will ever get to actually witnessing one myself!"

Nayidia sighed. "Well, all right; it is part of your history, after all." She smiled and commenced her tale.

"Many generations ago, a human king sat in his harbor, and wished for something he could do to make the world a better place. He wished upon a star moving through the night sky—"

Ylaine grinned; she knew what came next. "But it wasn't a star," she finished.

Nayidia nodded. "It wasn't; the small light came down to greet the king, and it was a fairy. The fairy told the king of a second kingdom, one under the water, whose inhabitants could only surface under the light of the Great Moon—"

"The Merfolk!" Ylaine crowed, wriggling all the way down to the tip of her fluke.

"The Merfolk," Nayidia confirmed. "That night was not a Great Moon, but because the human king had wished out of a pure heart, the fairy was able to use her magic to grant that wish. She brought the Mer-king—your grandfather—out of his castle, and the three realms created a pact: each Great Moon Rising, if the humans would gather at the harbor, the Merfolk would come and make gifts of rare seabed items that the humans could not make, the humans, in turn, would give the Merfolk foods and promise protection and safety over their domain—and the Fairies would give special, magical gifts to citizens of both realms."

Ylaine grinned and her eyes danced as images of seeing real-live fairies up close danced through her imagination. "But not everyone got a gift, right?"

"You are exactly right, Kelpling; you see, there were more humans and Merfolk than fairies, yet each fairy only had one gift to give; therefore, the fairies would decide who among the humans and the Merfolk were most in need of their gifts, and those would be given."

"Even my gift?" Ylaine asked mischievously, even though she knew the answer.

Nayidia tilted her head. "Your gift was special. You see, you were born just moons before the Great Moon Rising—I remember it well! But when we arrived, there were no humans gathered at the harbor, and only one lone fairy waiting for us on the surface of the water."

Ylaine felt the keen sting of disappointment; she didn't particularly like this part of the tale. "Is it really because of the humans?"

Nayidia flicked her tail emphatically. "The human king had banished the fairies, breaking the pact between us without any kind of trial or discussion. That is the only reason there were not more fairies, and no more gatherings after that. The Queen's selfless request came out of a pure heart, so the fairy bestowed her gift—the last fairy gift—on her infant daughter."

Ylaine felt the warm rush of happiness in thinking of her selfless mother. "Did you meet the water-fairy during one of the Great Moon Risings, Nayidia?"

Nayidia smiled and welcomed the change in tone. "Not I, Kelpling! A water-fairy gave the gift of magic to my own godmother, and she taught it to me when she saw I was ready to learn—and now I can use it to help you!" she declared proudly.

Ylaine stared with renewed admiration at the Mermaid who had been so like a mother to her. Never had Nayidia even hinted at such power. Why now? "So can you?" Ylaine asked. "Take away the songs?"

Nayidia settled comfortably on the bed once more. "I can do anything, my dear. Just for you—your birthday is coming, is it not?" She smiled benevolently.

"Oh yes, a few moons from now. Oh! That reminds me: father is always sad on my birthday, and I must sing to cheer him up. It's the only time he ever listens to me." Ylaine felt the agony of seeing her one chance to live normally slipping from her grasp. As much as her gift felt like a curse, she could not afford giving it up just yet.

Nayidia nodded wisely. "Better not take your voice then; the poor king would have to deal with his grief all on his own! I would not want to rob you of this chance."

Ylaine saw her chance slipping; her mind spun. "But—"

"Yes?" Nayidia prompted. "Something else you've always wished for?"

Her words awoke a thrill inside Ylaine, opened a desire she had tucked away forever. But Nayidia did say she could do anything, right?

"Well..." Ylaine confessed slowly, fighting to find the right words. "I've always... I mean, I have dreamed about... I sometimes imagine... being human." There! She said it!

Nayidia blinked. "Human?"

"Just for a day!" Ylaine pleaded.

Nayidia blew a scornful stream of bubbles. "A day? What do you expect to accomplish in such a short time? True love?" She rolled her eyes.

"Oh! Nothing like that." Ylaine hastened to explain. "You see, I have always imagined my father and I becoming humans for one day, and visiting Overcliff, and I would prove to him that the humans are still very ignorant of the Merfolk, and that they are peace-loving, and maybe—" her voice dropped under the weight of the hope that went with it, "maybe he'll call off the war."

At once, Nayidia's scoffing gave way to sympathy. She wrapped her arms around the young Mermaid and drew her close. "Oh, you poor thing! I see how much this means to you. I'll tell you what: I can brew two potions, one for you, and one for your father, that will give you both human bodies for one day."

Ylaine looked up at Nayidia, who stared back genuinely. "Really?" asked the Princess.

Nayidia nodded eagerly. "As a birthday present."

Ylaine was so excited she turned circles in the water. "Oh, Nayidia, thank you!" She gushed.

Nayidia began fussing about like a persnickety remora. "I'm afraid I can't allow you to visit me while I make them, but just as soon as they are done, on the day of your birthday, I will visit the palace to deliver them.

How does that sound?" She paused in her activity and glanced up at the young princess.

Ylaine nodded. "That sounds wonderful! Thank you so much!" She swam down and gave her nurse an enthusiastic hug. "You are a wonderful godmother!"

Nayidia laughed and peeled away. "Go on, little guppy; frolic and play!" She waved as Ylaine swam back toward the palace. "I will see you in a few moons!"

Ylaine's heart was full as she laid in her bed that night. Finally, her lifelong wish would come true!

Chapter 3

The Witch and The Storm

Alone in the hull of the ship, Nayidia watched the circling sharks overhead. They were strange creatures, sharks. So terrible in appearance, so menacing in their movements; but get to know a shark, and most of them were all heart and very little cunning. Like the hornshark that had tucked itself into the recesses of a disused cannon protruding from the last remaining gunwale. Its skeletal structure gave it a most sinister appearance. Nayidia swam to the cannon and gently coaxed the animal out of its nest. Humans were scared of all seakind except the ones that looked more scared of them.

"Naturally, they would think that a little thing like you would love nothing more than to tear into their soft pink flesh," she murmured, cradling the shark in her arm. She knew the truth: that the lazy, docile thing would rather snap at the tiny, soft-bodied organisms that happened to cross its path. He wasn't even big enough to cause lasting harm to a human—but the nature of its appearance frightened the foolish creatures.

She stroked its dorsal fin as it lay quietly. There wasn't even a thrash of alarm as the Mermaid suddenly gripped its tail with the hand beneath and ripped off its fin with her other hand. The spinal cord snapped, and the shark died instantly. Nayidia dug into its carcass with long, practiced fingers until she found the organ she sought. The remains she hurled into the open water, where a passing reef shark swallowed its kin.

Diving down into the lowest hull in the valley, Nayidia dropped the shark's liver into the cauldron she kept there. A keen light sparked in her icy blue eyes as she swam among the bottles and jars that looked to be discarded by the long-dead humans—as she had intended all along. The sea-witch poured the squid-ink into the cauldron and uncapped the hot spring underneath. The scalding water surrounded the cauldron in a bubble of near-vapor. It was good to be back.

"The little Mermaid wants to be human to prove something?" She sneered to herself as she cast spices and spells into the cloud of underwater steam. "The brave little princess wants to stop a big, awful war?" Nayidia felt her pent up frustration exploding out of her like the heat now leaching from the very earth's mantle, through the vent. "Does she have any idea what this is really about?" Nayidia left the foaming cauldron and returned to the top deck. The sharks still patrolled the area, but steered clear of the witch. Her three braids spread out from her head, waving about in the current like eels. She could barely see the tallest spire of Undersea Palace from here. The innocent little guppy who thought she could make her father see. Nayidia wanted to burst with loathing.

"Davor wants the one thing he can never have," she seethed. "Power; yes, he is King, but look at him! He can't even speak to his own council, he has to use his daughter to do it! Well, Davor," she muttered to herself. "Soon you will no longer have your little mouthpiece, and then where will you be? What power would you wield then?" Nayidia paused. The doll—the human doll with its ridiculous covering, made in the image of the land-walkers and yet having no automation of its own—lay where Ylaine had placed it. The witch swam to retrieve it.

"The Doll King will have no one to make him go or do," she said, stroking the stiff, coral-like cheek. "And so he will sit, in his palace, on his throne—" her hands trembled as they squeezed the small body. "Waiting, just waiting for the power to happen upon him until—" With a muted snap the body shattered in her hands. Pieces dropped to the seabed, most of them tangled in the folds of the dress. Nayidia still held the head. She turned it over. Peeking through the neck, she could see the backs of its glass eyes; the head held nothing—until Nayidia crammed a sea urchin into the void. Two spikes pressed against the right eye until it popped free of the socket, letting the spines protrude to create a gruesome visage.

"Until the one with true power takes the kingdom from he who is not fit to rule," she finished. Swimming down to where the pieces of doll had landed, Nayidia retrieved two of the shards—those imbecilic flat feet—and brought them to the cauldron. After carving five toes into the hard surface of each foot, she released them into the cloud.

"And when that time comes," she whispered, "I will be ready."

Satisfied that the potion was underway, Nayidia retrieved one more bottle. This did not contain any sort of vile substance, but instead, a piece of parchment bearing a list of explicit instructions, addressed to "Her Majesty, The Queen of Crossway." She had hoped to save this for the time when Davor actually declared war on Overcliff, but perhaps setting up her own welcoming committee to distract the human king and intimidate the Merking wasn't an altogether terrible idea.

Nayidia swam with this bottle up to the rocky crags of the mainland, far on the other side of the channel from Overcliff. She entered a small, mostly-submerged cove, and reached a hand out of the water to grasp the branch she felt there. Pulling it toward herself, Nayidia wrestled the entire shrub into the water. The twigs bit into her air-dried hands unmercifully, but she submerged them till the pain subsided. Nayidia tucked the bottle with the letter into a designated nook, where her contacts were sure to find it, and then swam back out to the channel. Just before she dived, Nayidia noticed an odd sight: four humans climbing into a small boat. Since the decline of the human kingdom, the number of boats had dwindled to just a few for the King's Armada; it was rare to see any fishing boats or small dinghies like this one, in spite of what King Davor thought. Nayidia noticed something striking about the features of one human in particular. It put her in the mind of the olden days, conducting business with the royal family of Overcliff. Surely that generation must have died out by now! Nayidia ducked quickly as the human in question suddenly turned in her direction.

Something about the man...

Nayidia smiled and returned to her lair. She selected her ingredients carefully; it wasn't the plan she had, but it would work just as well, perhaps even better. There was just one more spell to work.

❧ ❧

On the surface, Prince Nathan, his good friend Tom, the young lad Simon, and Tom's friend Dan all climbed into the Prince's sailboat for a brisk blow down the channel and back.

Nathan hopped into the boat first, and clapped a sea-captain's hat upon his head.

"All right you scallywags!" He bellowed with a grin. "I'm the captain and this is my ship, so you must do as I say! Dan and Tom," he pointed to the stern. "You'll sit there and be the navigators. Simon," he clapped the boy on the shoulder, "you'll sit in the prow with me."

The boys all entered into the game, laughing as they saluted. "Aye-aye, captain!"

Tom weighed anchor, and Dan steered the small sailboat out into the channel.

Nathan plopped onto the cushion next to Simon and tipped the hat back on his head. "Ahh, this is the life, isn't it?" he sighed. "I'm going to miss being able to do whatever I want like this when I am King!"

Dan teased, "Doesn't a king get to do whatever he pleases?"

Nathan shrugged. "I suppose—but it seems like Father just sits in court and reads proposals all day long." He snorted. "Looks rather boring to me!"

Out of all the group, Simon behaved least comfortable; he sat stiffly, eyes on the water instead of the boat, as if he wished the water to keep its distance. "I suppose a king must give up some pleasures for the good of his kingdom," he muttered softly.

Nathan chuckled. "I'll say!"

Tom tacked the sail and moored the line. "Speaking of pleasures," he announced, "you seemed to give up on our hunting trip pretty quickly, Nathan."

Nathan tilted an eyebrow and gestured to the sailboat. "I changed my mind, obviously! Besides, the game warden said there were only birds left in the forest now, and that struck me as far too much work for so little meat."

Simon's lips twitched. He watched the prince with a serious expression. "You know, most families on my side of the island would be glad of even a few sparrows."

Nathan chuckled. "You're kidding! Sparrows?" When no one joined in his laughter, he stopped and frowned at Simon. "What are you talking about?"

"Haven't you heard?" Simon tilted his head and his voice grew louder. "Food in the outer villages is getting more scarce all the time; the last harvest barely lasted through the winter, to say nothing of having enough to even think of planting for this year."

Nathan squirmed at the idea that there would be farms without food this harvest. "Well," he blustered, "the villagers can go ahead and hunt sparrows in the forest all they like!" He waved a hand to signal an end to this uncomfortable topic and asked Simon with a casual air, "How are you enjoying your studies at University?"

Simon turned away without answering as a red flush of embarrassment crawled up his cheeks. Nathan peeked over his shoulder, and saw Tom and Dan exchange an awkward glance.

"What is it?" he demanded.

Simon cleared his throat and squared his shoulders. "I… I'm no longer attending classes at University."

Nathan squinted in confusion. "Why not?"

Simon sighed. "Well, before the last term, my mother fell ill, and I had to stop attending lectures or risk losing the roof over my head."

Nathan gave him a friendly nudge. "You should have told me!" he chided. "I would have arranged for the University to give you a room and a bed."

"And what of my family, Prince?" Simon's face still bespoke pain. "I meant what I said literally—if I had not been there to fix the roof, our house would have fallen apart right over the top of us. My sisters are still young; they cannot make repairs and clean the barn and keep food on the table—I must do those things, because I am the man of the house." He hung his head shamefully. "That's what I have been doing with the money you send."

Tom, ever the positive one, spoke up. "Look at it this way, Nathan—at least your money is still going to a good cause."

Nathan welcomed the change in mood. "That's true!" he nodded. To Simon he said, "I'll tell the University to keep your desk open; I'm sure things will get better."

Simon shook his head. "But that's the trouble, isn't it?" He looked up at Nathan with a keen spark in his eye. "Things *aren't* getting better—and they haven't been at all good for some time. If anything, they will certainly get worse."

"What do you mean?" Nathan recoiled. "Why would you say that?"

Simon's lips pinched in a scowl as he pointed back toward the harbor they had left. "Look around!" he cried. "Don't you wonder why this boat is the only small craft left on the island? Overcliff used to export fish to the mainland on a regular basis—so where are all the fishing boats?"

"Well, I suppose—" Nathan started, but Simon cut him off.

"I'll tell you where they went! This last winter got so bad that all of Overcliff's fishermen—*all* of them—either sold their boats as firewood to families who had no kindling, or they chopped up the boats themselves."

Tom and Dan sat in stunned silence, but Nathan still tried to diffuse the tension. "More's the pity!" he cajoled with a shrug. "But then again, I guess it just means we get the whole channel to ourselves!" He stretched his arms and yelled at the top of his lungs to illustrate his point.

Simon still frowned. "You may joke, your Highness," he continued quietly, "but outside your warm, solid fortifications and beyond your high, stone walls you will find that Overcliff is dwindling away around you—"

"That's enough!" Nathan finally snapped, jabbing a finger at the young man. "I don't want to hear any more of it." He pulled the brim of his hat low over his face and rolled over to face the other direction from his three friends. The shade helped him forget the troubling revelations. The sun was warm, the movement of the boat peaceful and gentle as a cradle—

Nathan jumped awake as a splash of water hit his arm. He glared at Dan.

"What gives?" He complained.

Dan glanced up at him. "What are you talking about? I didn't do anything."

Just then, Nathan noticed that it was getting very dark, very quickly.

"Uhh," Simon stammered behind him, "guys?"

Nathan turned to see the biggest, blackest storm cloud he had ever witnessed billow out of a clear sky, blotting out the sun and pouring rain into the channel. The sail snapped crazily, and with a quick ripping sound it became a pathetic-looking flag of truce waving at the angry sky.

"ROW!" Nathan screamed, and Tom and Simon grabbed the oars from the bottom of the boat. The sea churned and swelled, burgeoning against the sides of the narrow channel like a restrained dragon. The waves carried the little boat so high that for a dreadful minute, their view of the dock was obscured by a wall of water. Then they began to descend.

"Hang on!" Yelled Nathan, but before he could follow his own advice, a sudden jerk twisted the boat out from under him, sending the young man high into the air. Nathan hit the water hard, and began sinking faster than he could swim upward. His lungs ached for breath. Blackness crept into his vision—but not before he glimpsed what looked to be a woman's face, filled with fear and moving toward him very fast. The blackness consumed him as strong arms wrapped around his waist.

కాలి తెలి

Prince Nathan sat at the window again, overlooking the Channel. From his room he could see the rock on which one of his father's soldiers discovered him. His three friends were dead. How had he been the only survivor?

His father—once he had gotten over his worry for his son's survival—had questioned him closely about how he had ended up there.

"Am I to understand," King Theodore said, when Nathan had told everything he knew, "That you lost consciousness while sinking in the water, and then somehow miraculously floated back to the surface to be washed up onto the rock where we found you? When every other man in the boat was dashed against the rocks and perished?"

Nathan knew how improbable it might sound, but how could he convince his father that this was the unvarnished truth? "Yes, you may understand that," Nathan replied, "If you refuse to hear the part where I describe the pale girl with the streaming hair who was in the act of swimming toward me when I blacked out."

"Ah yes," King Theodore retorted, "the deep-sea woman; tell me again! What did her eyes look like?"

"Like pale-green sea glass," Nathan's voice softened as he spoke of it.

"And her hair?"

Nathan frowned, "Some strange color; I couldn't tell because it was all behind her and my vision darkened. I would know it if I saw it again."

"And her face?"

Nathan wistfully began staring at the Channel again. "She was terrified," he whispered.

"That Channel is too dangerous for any subject of mine," King Theodore stated. "It is good that we need worry about patrolling it no longer."

Nathan's head snapped around and he frowned. "Why not?"

Theodore smiled and held up a letter bearing the royal seal of Crossway.

"Queen Devaine of Crossway has just sent this letter to inform me that she is willing to combine our kingdoms into one."

"You would surrender Overcliff to her, father?" Nathan queried incredulously. "Just like that?"

Giles stepped forward from where he had been leaning against the Prince's armoire.

"A treaty between kingdoms doesn't necessarily mean surrender, as one who has lost a war, Prince. There are other ways of negotiating the combination of thrones."

Nathan raised his eyebrows skeptically. "Such as?" He prompted his steward.

Giles shot a quick glance in the king's direction as he answered, "The simplest, of course would be marriage."

"Marriage?" Nathan cried with a grimace. He turned to his father, "You would marry the Queen?"

Theodore wrung his hands and shuffled nervously. "Well, not if it would displease you—"

"It would indeed."

"The Queen has a daughter."

The confusion returned. "So?"

"About your age, son."

"Me? Why would I want to marry some princess I have never met?"

"Now, Nathan, you must admit this day has always been

coming. You are fast becoming a man, and soon enough you will inherit the throne and crown of Overcliff."

"Not too soon!"

Theodore sighed. "Son, please listen! Overcliff is struggling and soon there will be nothing left. I fear I can do but little good for these people, feeble as I am. They need a strong leader to step forward and take command, to help the people and the land flourish once more!"

"I don't want to be King yet, father! I'm not ready!"

"Learn of it from Giles! He can teach you all that you need to know concerning laws and taxes, battle and strategy."

Nathan moaned and rolled his eyes.

"Nathan," Theodore abruptly drew himself to his full height with a steely glint in his eye, "The Queen and Princess are coming to negotiate the treaty in three days. Until then, you will learn exactly what you must know to be King from Giles, and when the Princess arrives I expect you to be the perfect gentleman and host to her as your guest."

Nathan rarely saw his father deliver commands like this, so whenever it happened, he knew resistance was useless. He hung his head. "Yes, Father." He looked up hopefully, "But what about the girl who—"

"No!" barked Theodore sharply. "You will not speak of girls in the water or magic beings of any kind. You merely had an accident, and as far as anyone knows, you swam into that rock yourself. Is that understood?"

"Yes, Father."

Theodore left the room. Giles waited in silence for a long moment before venturing to speak.

"Your highness—"

"Oh, go away, Giles!" Nathan snapped impetuously.

Giles bowed and took his leave.

Nathan threw himself on the chair at the window again. Would he ever find the girl who saved his life, or did she exist only in his mind and heart?

Chapter 4

Nayidia's Bargain

Unbeknownst to the Prince, the maiden who saved his life now swam in agitated little circles, deep in the water directly below his window.

Ylaine could not keep still as her insides flexed and knotted like a frightened octopus had taken residence in her belly.

She had saved a human. She, Princess Ylaine the Mermaid, had defied her father's command when she saw the body sinking in the water. Davor's Daughter had swum to the human, instead of letting him fall to her, and had lifted him up onto a rock at the middle of the channel, where she knew he would be rescued. Of course, her father's soldiers had set upon her almost at once, but at least she had been returning by then, and the matter stood. He would live because of her! Ylaine shook all over with excitement. The muscles she had felt as she carried him were so much different than the smooth, sleek tendons of the Merfolk. The legs had fascinated her. She saw that humans indeed had toes, just like Nayidia had said. They also had a strange kind of gill on their face, that was hard and bony and stuck out, instead of lying flat like slits. She had seen his eyes before the water closed them. She would never forget those eyes, staring down at her from the murky water.

Ylaine swam quickly back to her room, but even then, she could not relax. A cold hand of doubt seemed to encase her heart: Should she tell her father? What if she did? Would he believe her, that having an ally on the shore would mean they could have a human speak for them, removing the necessity for war and subjugation? Perhaps not; Ylaine knew her father was the sort who would use such an "ally" as more of a spy. Telling him about the human might cause anger because of her perceived betrayal, and it might cause the war to happen faster!

But maybe... If Ylaine found the man first...

She could convince him to get the King to make peace with the Merfolk. Or even if she could not manage that much, at least she would have the chance to meet him.

She would be gliding through the town, perfectly poised and radiating her beauty. As she paused to admire herself in a mirror, a deep, resonant voice like her father's would say, "Excuse me, have we met?"

She would turn around, and the moment their eyes met, she would know it was him. In her mind's eye, she saw the same wet, torn shirt, the silver clasp on his belt, and the clothes covering his legs, with his long feet exposed at the end. For some reason she couldn't see past the dark, short hair plastered against his pale face as water streamed over his closed eyes—but she firmly believed the connection they had would be undeniable.

"Oh my!" she would say, putting her hands up to her face. "I did not believe you would remember me."

"Come now," he would say, "I must know!"

"Well," she would waver slowly, giving him plenty of time to admire the way she moved so gracefully, "I saved your life once."

"By the Great Moon!" (a Merfolk expression—but surely humans used it too!) *"I have never stopped thinking about you since that moment." He would drop to one knee and seize her hand in his big, strong, warm ones, "From this moment forward, I pledge my life to you, and I swear to love you forever!"*

Giggling softly, Ylaine glanced at herself absently in the obsidian. Her hair threaded around the currents in a braid, which was unusual; instead of seaweed, she wore some kind of other, silky ropes. What were they? She pulled one out of her hair. It was long, wide, and flat.

"Ribbons," Ylaine whispered the foreign word. She looked up and toward a certain ship graveyard as her discussion and the agreement with her godmother came rushing back. "Nayidia's potions!"

The old Merwoman could not know what a gift she would now be giving Ylaine, the chance to meet the man she had saved! She froze in mid-celebration. "But what if one day is not long enough to find him?" And with her father no less? No! She could not bear the thought of never seeing him again! There was only one thing to do. Ylaine ignored the guard coming to summon her to dine with her father and swam back to Nayidia's place.

⁂

Nayidia was searching for trinkets among some of the outlying wrecks when she heard a voice calling out to her. Even from that distance, the voice seemed to strike a chord somewhere inside Nayidia. At once she was overcome with a sense of urgency that was more annoying than pertinent. She knew it was only Ylaine's voice that was doing this—and there was only one reason, Nayidia knew, why the Mermaid would be so agitated as to use her gift so senselessly. She swam to the anxious young princess at her own pace, exhibiting her resilience in spite of the pervading influence.

"Kelpling!" She greeted Ylaine as if the visit came as a surprise. "The potions are not ready yet, dear; did

I not say I would bring them to you myself?"

Ylaine still wore the braid Nayidia had woven herself, albeit a bit disheveled now, as she clutched the ribbon in her hands. Her dark tail flicked almost involuntarily.

"Can you make it longer?" She asked abruptly.

"Make what longer?" Nayidia pressed. She had to give the young Mermaid credit for figuring her new problem out so swiftly.

"Can you make one of the potions last longer? One day is not enough for me!"

"My dear, whatever can you mean? I thought you merely wanted to show your father the human world." Ylaine might have been clever, but Nayidia was exponentially more so.

Ylaine fluttered her gills and crossed her arms, gripping her shoulders in emotional distress. "Something has happened, Nayidia." She suddenly reached out and took Nayidia's hand in both of her own. "Something incredible." Her aqua eyes danced.

Nayidia did not have to fake the smile. She knew that Ylaine had no reason to suspect her level of enthusiasm as she prompted, "Dear one, tell me everything!"

So Ylaine treated Nayidia to the story of how she came to rescue the human. On the outside, Nayidia was just as astonished as a Mermaid should be; on the inside, she was fairly turning circles with glee. Her plan was working out so much better than she expected.

"—So you see, that's why I need more than one day, because I want to find him, Nayidia!" Ylaine's voice pleaded with her. "I need to find him."

The timbre resonated with ardent longing that told the Merwoman that her goddaughter's heart was already hovering on the surface of the water. Time for her body to join it.

"And what will you do when you find him, Ylaine?" Nayidia asked carefully.

The fluttering of the gills was the Mermaid equivalent of a blush. "I don't know." Ylaine looked as if she wanted to loose her hair and let it float in front of her face to avoid her godmother's gaze.

Nayidia let Ylaine wonder for several minutes, and then said slowly, as if the idea had just occurred to her, "I am afraid I cannot make the potions last any longer, but I do have some old three-day potion." Nayidia swam down to the belly of her ship to retrieve the vial of potion.

Ylaine was so excited to receive it that she did not notice the sparkling sheen of a fresh-brewed potion. "Three days?"

"Yes; you'll be human for three days—unless..." Nayidia broke off just long enough for Ylaine to look up expectantly, then shook her head. "Never mind, it's silly."

"What is?" Ylaine took the bait as easily as a tarpon.

"Well," Nayidia rolled her eyes, "there is an old legend that states that if a Mermaid becomes a human temporarily, and finds love in that time, she can stay human for as long as that love lasts."

"Really?" the younger Mermaid gasped. She wondered if a rescue warranted love to a human. Certainly she would not object if he offered!

"But I said it was silly; I mean, humans don't live that long, and they are fickle. You probably couldn't find someone in three days who would love you forever."

Ylaine stared at the potion in her hands. "But ... But I could try," she whispered.

Nayidia watched her young charge. "You really want to do this?"

Ylaine nodded, "I do."

Nayidia swallowed back her laughter. It was just too perfect! "I must warn you, Ylaine, that this potion isn't cheap. I'm afraid it will cost you something."

Ylaine frowned in confusion. "I thought you said you would give it as a birthday present."

Nayidia shook her head. "That was the one-day potion for you and your father. It's not ready yet, but I'd still give it to you in two more days, like I promised. If you take this potion now, though, I won't be able to do that."

Ylaine's lips trembled as she stared at the vial in her hand. "What do you want from me?"

"Come now, Kelpling," Nayidia responded smoothly, "it's not like that! I don't want anything from you, this is just an exchange, magic for magic."

Ylaine looked back to Nayidia. "What magic?"

Nayidia swam over to her cache of magic stones and chose a deep-green one. "Remember when we spoke, when I told you that I could temporarily remove your fairy gift? I was thinking that would be a fine bargain; I mean, I'll bet it only works in the water, anyway. It's not like you'll ever need it while you're human."

Ylaine hovered, mulling this over. "Won't that take away my voice?" She observed.

Nayidia bobbed her head. "No, it shouldn't; after all, you were born with a voice. The fairy only gave you the gift of song." She held up the green stone in her hand. "This stone can hold the gift for you. Can we try it?"

Ylaine squared her shoulders resolutely. "Go ahead," she answered.

Nayidia held the stone against her cheek and muttered the spell. A thin, glowing ribbon seeped out of Ylaine's mouth and entered the stone. The Merprincess clutched her throat as if Nayidia had just ripped out her tongue.

Nayidia chuckled, "Oh come now! It can't be that bad; try speaking."

Ylaine felt her gills flex convulsively as she struggled to get the words out. "I-I th-th-think it-t-t w-w-work-ked."

She yelped soundlessly and clapped a hand over her mouth. Ugh! Without the gift her voice hung flat and ungainly, and that stutter!

Nayidia didn't seem to notice as she tucked the stone into a small pouch made of woven kelp at her side. "You'll get used to it after a while, I'm sure," she told the young Mermaid. "Don't worry about your gift. I'll keep it safe and give it right back when you return."

Ylaine did not want to have to hear her voice again, but she had to remind her godmother. "B-b-but-t i-if I f-f-find l-l-love, I w-won't b-be b-b-back."

Nayidia frowned as if recalling this for the first time. "Ah, I see; well, here's what we can do." She swam out to another ship covered over with smooth, round shells like large pearls. Picking one, she handed it to Ylaine. "This is called a mier. When the shell is struck, it makes a sound only Merfolk can hear. Watch." Nayidia smacked the mier on the side of the ship, and a piercing shriek echoed through the water.

"If you find your love and are sure you're not coming back in three days, just place the mier in water and strike it, and I will swim up to you and return your gift. Does that sound all right to you?"

Ylaine nodded wordlessly.

Nayidia smiled, "Enjoy your three days, Princess. Oh, and one more thing: the potion will begin to work right away, so you'll want to swim as near the surface as you can get before taking it. Wouldn't want you drowning before you used your legs properly, now would we?"

Ylaine frowned with worry. Rescuing the human had been the first time she had made it all the way to the surface, and even then she barely had time to ease his unconscious body onto the rock before the guards were upon her, forcing her back within the shining barrier. To be able to escape, then, was not just a matter of getting to the surface.

"H-how-w w-ill-l I g-g-get t-to sh-sh-ore?" It took all her concentration to enunciate one sentence.

Nayidia gave a reassuring smile. She beckoned to the Princess. "Follow me."

Nayidia and Ylaine swam along the sea bed till they reached a high cliff that Ylaine recognized as the foundation of Overcliff. The boundary stretched high overhead, but in the murk of the water, Ylaine saw a round cave cut into the side of the rock. Nayidia pointed to it.

"That is a tunnel that will take you to the surface just meters away from a small harbor. Just swim through there and take the potion when you get to the other side. The boundary guards never swim that far."

Ylaine was so excited that she threw her arms around Nayidia.

"Th-th-thank-k y-y-you!" She spluttered.

"For you, my Kelpling," Nayidia murmured, "anything."

Her heart nearly bursting with hope, Ylaine swam to the cave and entered the tunnel.

Nayidia returned to her lair. Soon enough, Davor would notice his daughter missing, and of course he would come immediately to her. Nayidia twirled her braids as she invented the perfect cover story. So far, the whole plan ran along smoothly. Davor would rue the day he ever thought he could rule the ocean all on his own.

Chapter 5

Fish out of Water

Ylaine slowed as she wove her way through the tunnel. The vial of potion glinted off various heaps of things like pearls and sea-gems scattered over the floor of the tunnel. Had she known of such things, she would have realized that this was an old smuggling tunnel some of the more self-interested Mer-traders would use to reserve amounts of rare sea-goods for trading, and also to reach the surface before the official delegations could make the journey through the open water.

Just when Ylaine was beginning to question the validity of her plan, and to consider turning back, she saw the end of the darkness ahead.

Her tail quivered as she swam into the open water. The King's Boundary was behind her! She was free! Ylaine looked up to the surface, just a few meters away. She now hovered on the far side of the island of

Overcliff, where the rocky cliffs opened up to a stony beach and a series of wooden posts, with boards between them. Nayidia had said once that humans walked on these to be near the water but staying out of it, since they breathed air, not water. Without gills, the water would drown them. Ylaine swam as far as the posts that supported the walkway. She figured she would be able to climb up quick enough. Her tail fluttered at the thought of what was to come; when she came free of the water, would she finally get to fly?

Ylaine positioned herself just below one of the walking places. Bracing herself, she uncorked the bottle and poured the potion into her mouth.

It blazed like the sting of a sea urchin all the way down her throat. As the potion entered her belly, Ylaine felt a strange feeling in her throat, as if her gills had suddenly seared shut. Water was coming in—but she could no longer breathe! Desperately, she shoved her face against the walk-place, gasping the air above the water for the first time.

But the potion had not finished. The stinging pain seemed to seep right past her stomach, all the way down to her tail—and right down the middle of that to her fin. The potion cut her tail in two like a shark's bite, ripping into flesh and bone. Ylaine could not even scream as the long fin folded on itself, her spine twisting as length was lost. She felt the flexibility of her tail stiffening into rigid, jointed legs and feet. Frantically, she reached up and pulled her head above the water. Heaving, spewing, the former Mermaid filled fresh lungs with gasps of real air.

She clung to the post with her head barely above the water, taking quick gasps as she learned to use her new lungs. Something brushed her fin—*foot*, she corrected herself—and she looked down to see a massive white object floating to the surface. The dress! She recalled Nayidia mentioning that all humans wore clothes. Ylaine figured her godmother must have sent it up after her. The young former Mermaid reached out her hand and pulled it toward herself. Keeping her legs wrapped around the post, she worked the dress onto her body. Once clothed, Ylaine gripped the walkway with her hands and gave a great heave. For the first time in more than a century, a Mermaid rose completely out of the water and took her first tentative steps on land.

On the road into town, Ylaine struggled to maintain her balance with only a tall pole for support. She was getting used to being dry, used to her hair hanging down her back instead of up around her head (and the fact that it was now the color that her tail had been).

As the sheen of water faded from her skin, Ylaine discovered the first flaw in her assumptions about surface life: Humans did not float. They apparently did not even leave the ground very easily, shuffling along on their feet to get around. To her intense disappointment, walking was not at all like floating. Her feet stuck to the ground in a most aggravating manner, and her tall, bony body tilted precariously this way and that.

If this were the water, Ylaine thought, *I could just swim over the tops of these buildings till I saw the man I saved, and then dive right to him.*

However, the former Mermaid could not, and had to merely trudge along. Each step sent a jolt through her delicate body. She figured she probably looked like such a dolt that she might not have to worry about driving him away with her stutter; he'd see her coming and run of his own accord.

The next cause for disappointment came soon after her first steps. The more she walked, the more she became disgusted with her human body. It was not smooth and streamlined like a Merperson's body. A human woman's body, Ylaine decided, was lumpy: the arms, the chest, the legs. Everything bulged with muscles. The pointy blowhole did not seem to filter anything like gills did. How could anyone think that this was beautiful at all? What kept the humans upright, if they all had this terrible, dragging weight to them?

"Look out, girl!"

The harsh cry grated over Ylaine's ears, jerking her from the introspection. She shrieked as a large wagon pulled by a strange animal bore down on her. The staff fell from her grasp as she tumbled out of its path.

SPLAT!

Ylaine felt like she was back in the sea as she landed headfirst in a cart full of fish. She flailed her arms but the fish would not let her go. Unexpectedly, a human hand grabbed her and pulled, bringing her up and out of the cart. Ylaine frowned to see that the fish had left stains and slime on her dress.

"Hello, there!" A voice laughed.

Ylaine looked up. Her rescuer had dark hair and twinkling brown eyes. *Could it be?* Her heart wondered as he smiled at her. "Are you all right? That was quite a tumble!"

"Y-y-yes," she stammered. Her cheeks burned to hear her dead, clumsy voice—the reminder of what she had given up. All hope of finding the man she sought slowly began to deflate inside her; this wasn't the way it was supposed to happen, this was obviously the wrong man—now she wondered if it ever would. She turned and began to hobble away.

In three strides, the tall young human had caught up to her. "Have we met?" He asked abruptly.

Ylaine didn't trust herself to speak, so she only shook her head. She was quite sure he mistook her for another girl, a real human. *It couldn't be him!* She reminded herself. He didn't look anything like the human she had rescued—and he didn't sound like the right one, either!

Her companion shrugged easily in her silence. "Oh, don't worry, it'll come to me. What's your name?"

Oh gracious! She didn't know if she could manage her own name. Why couldn't he just go away?

"Y-y-la-laine-ne," she sputtered.

"What? Ill—Illeinina?" He mistook her stutter for extra syllables. "Hmph; is that all? Have you no other title or family name?"

She shook her head again; the only title she could claim would be Princess, but surely that did not matter here in the human kingdom. She could be plain Illeinina the human for as long as this form lasted.

"You must be poor, then," the young man continued bluntly.

The remark stung Ylaine; the royal coffers of Undersea made her richer than any human could ever hope to be! She turned to hide the flush of shame and did her best to flounce away from him in a huff. Never mind finding her human true love! They all looked the same anyway—right down to the cut of their hair, all short. At least Mermen with the same hair color typically wore it on their head at different lengths. The more she searched, the more she became convinced that all humans looked the same—they were all reflections of that aggravating, curious, arrogant young—guppy! Navigating the dirty, dry, streets took all of her concentration. Ylaine was careful to give a wide berth to everything around her, and shrunk back from the slightest noise. Once, a large animal let out a loud "Moooo!" just as she was very near, and Ylaine whirled away with a scream—

Right into the waiting arms of the young man.

"St-st-stop f-f-following-g m-me!" She spluttered.

He only laughed. "Oh come," he said with a merry twinkle in his eye, "who else would save you from the great and terrible milk cow?" He nodded toward the animal.

Ylaine frowned and tried to change direction once more. "I d-don't n-n-need y-you."

She and he were the same height, but he had more command over his legs than she did. He caught her again. "Illeinina, wait! Are you sure you have never been to one of my—of the palace's gala events?"

She jerked her hand away, "I h-have n-n-never-ver b-been t-t-to O-o-Over-c-cliff b-be-f-f-fore."

"Really?" The young man frowned. He surveyed the tattered dress and the tilting walk. "What are you doing here, then?"

"I n-n-need to f-f-find s-someb-b-body."

"Who is it?"

"N-none of y-y-your b-b-business!"

He still would not leave her side. "Illeinina—" he sighed. "Look, I'm sorry about the cow thing. That was unbecoming. Let me make it up to you: you could use a guide, since you're new here, so why don't I buy us a picnic, and after we eat, I'll help you find whoever it is you're looking for. Does that suit you?"

Ylaine almost refused him yet again, but she knew that what he said about a guide was true; maybe he even knew the man she sought. She had no idea what a picnic was, but it sounded like some kind of food, and she had not eaten since leaving the water. Finally, she nodded.

"Y-y...yes!" The word came out short and sharp, like the bark of a dog.

The man smiled and held out his arm to her. "I was hoping you'd say that," he said.

Ylaine wasn't sure what he was doing with his arm. She held hers up in the same way. Maybe this was a special way humans walked—

The young man laughed and took her left hand, bringing it through the crook of his arm.

"Pleased to meet you, Illeinina," he said. "My name is Nathan."

Ylaine soon discovered that "picnic" wasn't just one sort of food, it was many. Nathan led her among the stalls, trading pieces of gold for edibles, or letting Ylaine sample the more interesting ones. She found foods where you ate everything but the hard knob in the middle, foods you ate by the handful, foods that took two hands to hold while you ate, foods that you had to take off the outside before you ate—and every time, Nathan dispensed gold pieces like it was nothing. Coupled with the respect everyone showed him, Ylaine concluded that he must be very rich.

The pair withdrew to a pleasant hillside overlooking the town, and Nathan and Ylaine sat on smooth, flat rocks as they ate the bread, cheese, and peaches and drank jugs of fresh-pressed cider. Nathan kept talking all the while and made no remarks over her stutter, and Ylaine found that if she waited between words the stutter was not so pronounced. It took a long time to say anything at all, but Nathan always waited, watching her with that same intense gaze that was trying to place her in his memory. She wondered if the man she sought (if she ever found him) would show her the same tolerance and patience.

The conversation soon progressed to petty likes and dislikes. Nathan began to notice a pattern among the topics Illeinina chose.

"You must be from one of the sea-towns on the mainland," he guessed. "I'm betting your father is a fish merchant, am I right?"

Ylaine smirked shyly. "More...fish... than...m-merch-chant," she quipped, hoping that he would take it as the joke Illeinina the human would mean it for.

Nathan laughed. "That bad, huh? I understand." His face grew serious, "My father is too wrapped up in his work, too. Sometimes, I just want to get out of this place, and I wonder if my father would even notice if I was gone."

Ylaine's thoughts dipped briefly below the surface of the water, toward her own father; did he notice her absence?

"Anyway, I am still waiting for the right time, I guess," Nathan continued. "In all seriousness, Illeinina, I envy you; you come to my country having freely left your own to begin a fresh start in a whole new world. I wish I could have that chance!"

Ylaine couldn't help feeling that there was something familiar about the longing in his eyes as he spoke.

"Not...really," she spoke slowly, quelling the relentless urge to stutter over each consonant. "Truly... I...feel I... changed...so much th-that maybe...I...didn't leave... at all...but...that... someone...else... not...me... left...in my...place."

Nathan shrugged and drank from his jug. "That's an interesting point: why leave if you have to be someone other than yourself? I can't help feeling that I certainly wouldn't want to risk not being myself. I don't know; you seem like a genuine article to me. In fact—" he peered at her searchingly, "I could swear we've met somewhere before."

Ylaine blushed and dropped her eyes. How could he know the impossibility of such a thing?

Nathan soon dispelled her confusion. "Oh now I remember!" he cried. "You remind me of the girl in my dreams." He looked at her with eyes alight.

Ylaine glanced up in alarm. Could he—no! It couldn't be! "D-d-dreams?" she forgot all about covering her stutter.

Nathan shook his head. "Not like that!" He tried to explain, "Okay: a few days ago I was out boating with some friends. A storm hit and overturned our boat. We were all thrown into the water, and I thought I was going to drown…" his voice faded as the faces of his friends returned to haunt him. If only he had shown more care! He cleared his throat, but the lump remained.

"And just before the world went black…" Nathan at last recalled himself and stopped as Illeinina stared at him with eyes full of pity. "Never mind," he muttered, "I sound ridiculous."

Ylaine felt the realization flooding over her heart. "You…wonder…how… you… woke… up… on…. the… rock… in… the… Channel."

Nathan blinked in astonishment. "How did you— oh gods, you are her!" He seized Ylaine's hands with sudden energy. "You're the girl who saved me!" He reached up and smoothed her hair from her face. It was the same! The pale skin, the ethereal eyes! He had not recognized the raven-colored hair. "How can I repay you?" he gasped.

She blushed; wasn't that just what she wanted him to say? Why did she feel no welling of love between them, then? She just couldn't place him in her dream of the noble human willing to pledge his life for her. Especially when so many others drowned; why had she not saved them? Her plan to find love had failed utterly. "Well, you saved me at the market," she mumbled.

Nathan shook his head at the stuttering girl's modesty. "From the fish barrel?" he chuckled, "Come, that was nothing; I only rescued your dignity. That is far less than a life! I am still in your debt; tell me what you—"

"Your highness!"

The pair looked up as a well-dressed courtier approached from the road. He seemed to be waving to them—for a moment Ylaine wondered how a human could know she was a princess, but then Nathan was pulling her to her feet and straightening his appearance. He smiled as the courtier bowed. Suddenly the young lady felt her heart thudding within her as she realized she had grossly underestimated her new friend.

"On second thought," Nathan was saying with a grin, "I have an idea. How about a room at the royal palace?" He winked at her.

Ylaine's brain was spinning out of control. "P-p-p-p-palace! H-h-highn-n-ness!" She was so astounded that she would have run away, but he still held her hands. She did not know what to think. "Y-y-y-you! You're th-th-th-the-the—"

The courtier frowned at the stunned young lady in the tattered, sodden dress, and told Prince Nathan, "Your father requests that you return for supper, and to rehearse for when the Queen arrives tomorrow."

Nathan sighed and dropped Ylaine's hands to run his own through his hair. "Oh yes, the Queen." He sighed, "I'd forgotten about that."

The courtier couldn't help casting a worried glance toward the strangely tall woman behind the prince, who had ceased jabbering and lapsed into petrified silence. "I beg your pardon, Highness, but what is that?"

Nathan stepped aside and led Ylaine forward. "Don't be rude, Giles! I want you to give her a room, and servants, and dresses befitting a lady who saved the Prince's life!"

Giles' eyes opened wide. He had been among those concerned for the Prince's safety during the storm that claimed so many lives, and elated at his miraculous rescue. He now smiled at Ylaine. "Oh! Right this way, Milady!"

Hearing mention of her new friend's identity only sent Ylaine into another bout of stuttering. "Th-th-the-the-the p-p-p-p-p-p—"

Chapter 6

Lessons in Etiquette

That is how it came to pass that Ylaine the Mer-princess, not twelve hours out of the water, came to live at the palace. In no time at all she discovered that Giles had arranged to give her a room and a wardrobe full of dresses, and she overheard Nathan insisting that she be included in his lessons on matters of etiquette.

Giles objected at first. "Your highness, I hardly think a total stranger would be adequate training for you—

"It's *got* to be her, Giles," Nathan maintained, little knowing that the young woman in question stood just outside the door, listening to him. "I would rather practice my manners with Illeinina—"

"Who?"

Nathan sighed. "That's her name, and you must call her that, Giles, because I'm through having to sit through another giggle-infested gossip session with any more of those court ladies you've been drumming up!"

"But, your highness," Giles protested. "By all appearances she has never been to Overcliff before, and certainly she doesn't seem to come from any kind of civilized kingdom!"

"I don't know, Giles," Nathan mused. "Something about her—I always feel stiff as a pasteboard around the court, but talking with Ileinina… I just—"

"Oh, very well, Prince," Giles finally gave in. "We will begin tomorrow morning. But I am warning you, if I see that you are too busy indulging any kind of infatuation with this stranger—"

"Don't worry, Giles; I'm sure we'll both be on our best behavior."

Ylaine scurried back to her room in a turmoil of nervousness. Unfortunately, she found it full of even more people, who all stopped and nodded to her.

When Ylaine continued to stare in shock, the maid closest to her cleared her throat. "Milady, we have been assigned to your service by Master Giles. He has warned us suitably of your—" she faltered, "ahem, malady of speech, and therefore we shall endeavor to accomodate your wishes by the use of hand gestures and nods. If you please, madam, there are a few gowns here for you to try, as *that one*," she gazed at the frumpled, mildewed dress Ylaine wore, "is entirely unfit for dining with the King. When we have taken your measurements, the royal tailor will set about making your wardrobe, but until then, a borrowed dress will have to do." She paused and gave another curtsey. "Does this please you?"

Ylaine let her eyes travel over the assembly of maids—dedicated to assisting her, according to human customs—and she forced a little nod.

The matron smiled. "Then let us begin!"

The maids helped her into a gown of peacock-blue brocade trimmed in gold, which set off her eyes and pale skin. Two more maids combed out her luxurious dark hair and styled it around her head in a most becoming fashion.

Finally, they helped her stand and walk into the hallway where Prince Nathan waited. As much as she had been squeezed, pushed, jerked, and pinched by all these new things, Ylaine actually found that she could relax into the tiny steps the dress restricted her to, as it made her feel more sure of her footing instead of ready to fall over.

That moment when Prince Nathan turned and saw her all cleaned and human-looking was a sight Ylaine knew she would treasure for the rest of her life.

He grinned, but it wasn't the grin of amusement over her embarrassment. Ylaine wondered if it wasn't love in his eyes when he looked at her. He offered his arm as he had done in the marketplace, but this time Ylaine slipped her arm through his, the right way.

He laughed, "They must have some strange customs on the mainland, but you are learning ours quickly enough. My father awaits us in the Great Hall."

A fresh wave of apprehension washed over Ylaine as Nathan led her to the massive double-doors flanked by guards. How on earth was she going to impress the King with the horrible stutter she could never overcome? Nathan ignoring the impediment was fortunate enough; Ylaine doubted she could have the same luck twice.

∞☙ ❧∞

King Theodore sat at the head of the table. The smile he bestowed on his son faltered when he spotted the strange—albeit beautiful—girl behind him.

"Father," Nathan announced, bringing Ylaine forward, "I've found her."

"Found whom?" Theodore frowned in puzzlement. "My son, the table is laid, and you bring a guest?"

Nathan signaled a waiting footman. "Bring another place. She will dine with us."

Ylaine hesitated there at Nathan's side. She knew that the ruler of a kingdom deserved a demonstration of respect—but she had no idea how humans bowed. As a mermaid she would straighten her body, thrust her arms back and flutter her tail; as a human, her body was already straight, and she had no tail. On impulse, Ylaine bent her head toward the King and bent her body into a half-crouch, throwing one arm back and bending the other in front of her as she had watched Nathan do. She held this position till her legs began to wobble, then stood.

The King and the Prince just stared at her. Ylaine saw a smile play across Giles' mouth.

King Theodore blinked. "What is your name, my dear?"

Ylaine could feel her tongue seize; her mind fairly screamed the answer but her mouth would not move.

Nathan answered for her. "Her name is Illeinina—and she was the one who saved me from drowning."

Theodore started and nearly fumbled his fork. "Really? Hm, ah, yes.... Indeed; well, Lady Illeinina, you have the kingdom's profoundest gratitude. Please do sit and join us."

Nathan grinned at her as she sat before the plate.

"I hope you like it," he said, "being from a sea town and all."

Ylaine stared at the dish before her: a sea bass, filleted and roasted, still crackling from its brief respite in the castle ovens. Not that she had never consumed fish before; the big, flat tunas and the sleek eels were every bit as much a food source to the merfolk as cattle and fowl were to humans.

What puzzled her immensely was how to use the strange-shaped utensils laid all around her plate. All her life she had never used anything other than the fine-tipped whalebone skewers to either pinch or stab the food. These strange shapes—several with many stabbing points, one with a flat, smooth edge, and another that looked like a small sword—made the very act of eating seem like a complicated maneuver. Ylaine picked up the pronged utensil, watching Nathan's hands carefully out of the corner of her eye to see how it was used.

The King and Prince, for their part, did not notice their guest's predicament, instead conversing amongst themselves.

"I hope the arrival of this girl has not made you neglect the instructions I gave you, Nathan."

"Not a bit, Father! Giles still makes me sit while he throws figures at my head like knives at a target!"

"Oh? Then what have you learned about the nation of Crossway?"

"Well... erm..."

"If we are going to establish a treaty, son, I want you to know all about it."

"No, no; I remember. It's just..." Involuntarily, his gaze betrayed his thoughts and wandered to the girl beside him.

"Well?" Theodore recalled him to reality.

"Oh, er," Nathan stammered as both Giles and the King watched him from either side, "I know that the principal export from Crossway is fish and, um... Coral?"

"I believe the pearls are that kingdom's greatest treasure, but we will let that stand. Who rules Crossway?"

"Um, King—"

"Queen, son."

"Queen.... Davo-Davi..."

Theodore rubbed his brow. "Her name is Queen Devaine."

"Right."

Theodore cast a concerned glance in the direction of Giles. "I see that you have not been giving this kingdom the attention it deserves. Perhaps when the Queen arrives tomorrow I may have to—"

"No father!" Nathan begged. "I'll do better, I promise! It's just that, today, with Illeinina and all—"

"Is she too much of a distraction for you, Nathan?"

Ylaine could not restrain a hazarded glance; would she be sent away for his sake, so soon?

"No she is not," Nathan affirmed, even going so far as to take Ylaine's hand and clasp it reassuringly. "I will learn everything by tomorrow evening."

King Theodore snorted. "Hmph! See that you do."

Nothing more was said during the meal, but as they parted ways to retire for the night, Nathan put his arms around Ylaine's shoulders. She felt his warmth radiate from his core; she had never felt such a thing in the water.

"Now that I've found you, I will never send you away, Illeinina," he whispered in her ear, his breath pulsing against her skin. "I promise."

Her first morning as a human, Ylaine followed a servant sent to bring her to where Giles waited for her in the parlor.

Giles stood at the front of the room, facing the door, which is why he saw her before the Prince, who slouched in a high-backed chair facing him.

Giles smiled at the demure beauty. Wherever she had come from, she fairly effused gentility, not like any of the other "fishmongers' daughters" he had ever met. The fine clothes and appearance suited her perfectly.

"Ah," he said, striding over and taking her hand, "my Princess has arrived."

Ylaine nearly tripped over her own feet in alarm, and clutched at Giles' hand while her breath caught in her throat and her eyes flew open. How in the world did he know her secret?

"What do you mean, Princess?" Nathan asked, lazily tumbling to his feet. He smiled that same warm smile at Ylaine that he had given before.

"I mean," said Giles, turning to the Prince, "that lessons in etiquette are all well in theory and discussion, but there is no better teacher than practice, is there?"

Nathan took Ylaine's hand and led her to the sofa, allowing her to sit. He eyed his steward. "You know I hate it when you use ambiguous terms, Giles."

The steward snorted. "All this time I have been explaining to you how you ought to treat the Princess of Crossway when she arrives, and of course you've been paying attention," he laid particular emphasis on those words, which made Nathan flinch. "So, my prince: show me what you have learned."

Prince Nathan glanced around the room, as if he expected the Queen and her daughter to suddenly emerge from a hidden cupboard. "What, now?" He asked Giles.

The steward sighed. "Pretend for the day that Illeinina is Princess Melinda. How would you treat her?"

"Oh." As if hearing about another princess potentially requiring the prince's affections was not uncomfortable enough, Ylaine could not help but notice the way Nathan pulled away slightly from her when Giles compared her to this Melinda creature. Had they met before and it turned out badly?

"Let's begin." Giles would not be dissuaded. "Your Highness, allow me to present Princess Melinda of Crossway." He raised his eyebrows and nodded to Ylaine.

It was her cue! She nodded to the Nathan as Princess Melinda, and said, "Your Majesty."

Ylaine colored deeply at her flat, stammering voice as Nathan rolled his eyes at Giles. "This is never going to work!" He muttered.

"Ahem!" Giles peered at him severely. "First lesson: never let your true feelings show in the first meeting. Treat every lady like a radiant star, no matter what her faults or flaws."

Nathan tilted his head toward Giles and raised an eyebrow. Giles gestured for him to proceed.

Ylaine heard the Prince mutter, "Radiant star, got it..." under his breath. They locked eyes again. She felt her heart flutter just the tiniest bit faster.

"Princess Melinda," Prince Nathan said abruptly, "how good of you to grace our fair kingdom with your illustrious presence."

The flowery language was so stiff and puffed-up sounding that it made Ylaine giggle. In a burst of theatricality, she bounded to her feet and said, "Truly, I had only come to see with my own eyes if the rumors were true."

"Oh?" The Prince returned, warming up to the charade. "What rumors might those be?"

"Th-they say your people consider the sea as part of your domain, and thus all the fish belong to the King."

"And?" Nathan chuckled. "What of that? Certainly it's not the whole ocean, just as far as the armada can patrol."

"What armada?"

Giles interposed with a loud "Ahem! Lesson two: Emphasize the strengths to disguise the weaknesses. Your Highness, may I suggest offering your guest a tour of the best locations in the kingdom to steer the topic away from those things the kingdom lacks?"

The two seemed very comfortable speaking candidly in her presence; Ylaine did not mind. She was the very thing she wanted to be: a barnacle on the hull of the castle, observing human interactions firsthand.

"Right," Nathan said. "Ah, Princess, would you like a tour of the kingdom?"

She bounced in unfeigned excitement. "Oh, yes, indeed."

Nathan turned to his steward. "Giles, prepare the carriage."

Giles bowed with a grin. "There is already a chaise to convey you two waiting in the courtyard, your majesties."

Ylaine looked all around as they walked out through the atrium to the outer court. People bustled everywhere, dressed in royal livery. The erstwhile Mermaid saw humans of every shape, size, and shades of skin as varied as those of her own people, the greys and blues replaced by tans, olives, and browns. Contrary to the Merfolk, human hair seemed to be limited in the range of black, grey, golden, red, or brown. While the most colorful thing about a Merperson might be their hair or their tail, for humans all of that color was represented in their clothing. The bigger the human, the more cloth they wore, mounds of the stuff. Ylaine saw dresses that reminded her of the one she had borrowed from Nayidia. She saw simple ones, more like the dresses she had been wearing during her time at the castle.

The thing that struck her most was the profusion of smiles she saw in the areas near the palace. The humans all nodded pleasantly to one another, and their voices carried a sort of lilting cadence to them. Nathan escorted "Princess" Ylaine around to the different booths and stalls displaying wares from all around the mainland. A greasy head honing in very close to hers drew her attention away from exploring her surroundings with her eyes. Gnarled fingers picked up the golden cowrie around her neck as the jeweler examined it closely.

"That's rare seabed metal, that is," he whined. "Haven't seen the like in ages; there are precious few divers willing to risk the kind of death that awaits someone who tries to mine that stuff! If you don't mind my asking, where did you get it?"

Ylaine didn't like the greedy glint in the man's eyes; it made him look like an angry barracuda. She clasped a hand over her necklace and shrank away as Nathan told the man off.

"Sorry," he whispered as they continued.

Ylaine felt so violated that she nailed him with her

eyes and seethed, "If you're going to let the filthy merchants touch the princess—"

Nathan looked positively stricken. "Illeinina, I'm sorry! I didn't mean for that to happen."

Ylaine's heart still raced; if she had lost the cowrie shell, it would not matter if she was Mermaid or human—by law she would be barred from the palace, and who would ever accept former royalty into their home? The man's eyes had told her how much he wanted to steal it. She noticed that Nathan kept a better hold on her arm now, even clasping her hand in his.

They were leaving the vicinity of the palace now. Nathan wanted to show her the Carnival that practically lived on the island, giving shows every day, but Ylaine was noticing something else. Looking at nearby market stalls, at the people walking among them, she asked quietly, "Where are the smiles?"

"Come again?" Nathan finished laughing at a joke from the carnival buffoon and turned to her.

Ylaine pointed to a group of women perusing the goods for sale. Their expressions as they fingered the finery held wistfulness, and sadness when they looked in their near-empty baskets, and self-consciousness when they noticed a new stain or rip in their own clothes, and despair when they compared the prices for even basic goods to the meager contents of their coin purses.

"They aren't happy."

Nathan watched them. At first, he was inclined to regard them as "just people"—but Illeinina's words caused him to ponder: was it really something shocking to see unhappy people?

"Well, of course they are," he blustered, pushing her on toward the Arboretum that was a pet project of the Overcliff regents. Somehow it seemed smaller than he remembered. It troubled him. What had happened all this time?

Ylaine was still waiting for him to continue. Nathan grunted.

"Overcliff isn't a very large or affluent community; one cannot be pleased all the time. It is only natural that some may be facing difficulty at the moment. That's life, you know."

Ylaine looked around, even as Nathan led her to the most fantastic garden she had ever seen, in the water or out. But she could not forget the looks on all the faces in the village; such lines of heaviness and hollowness of the bodies bespoke years of hardship, not moments. Yet behind the palace walls, all was plenty and health and happiness.

Under the water, all Merfolk enjoyed a quiet existence, and plenty for all readily available for the gathering. What was it about this kingdom that they should run out of resources? How else could one explain the sharp contrast between two regions of the same kingdom?

Nathan tugged her down a side street. "This way," he said. "We have a university here on the island, and I used to study there. We should visit it."

They passed into a relatively cleaner part of town, but as with much of the other parts of the outer city, the streets were mostly devoid of people.

They reached the university, but Ylaine did not see any studying going on there.

Nathan paused, puzzled. "Hello?" he called.

Ylaine caught the frown. "What's wrong?"

Nathan walked up to the door. "It should not be empty right now..."

But there was a notice posted on the door. *"In knowledge there is life, and without knowledge, the people perish."* Below it, another sign: *"Give money to a fool and you will both die poor; he does not know how much he has, only that he can ask for more."*

"What does it mean?" asked Ylaine, but Nathan ushered her away from the door.

"Never mind," he said. "Let's go somewhere else."

Ylaine did not understand his reluctance. "What is wrong with the kingdom?" She asked. "Yesterday you talked as if royal life was nothing but a bore, because everything basically ran itself."

Nathan stopped and sat upon a crate. He ran his

hands through his hair.

"I don't know!" He admitted to her. "I don't know. Illeinina, I guess I always assumed that if things didn't change for me, then things weren't changing anywhere else." He glanced back toward the university. "But things were changing, and now..." Simon's last words came back to haunt him: *the kingdom is dwindling away...* " He had not wanted to think about it before, but now it fairly slapped him in the face; that would all change once they made the treaty with Crossway, wouldn't it?

Ylaine sat next to him and put her hand over his. "What will you do?"

Nathan stood and helped her to her feet. "Well, I have gotten by this long without having any changes.... I think it's time I started making some."

Together, they began the long walk back to the palace.

"What kinds of changes will you make?" She asked.

"I'm not sure yet," Nathan responded. "But I have a tutor who's been trying to get through to me, and I have a hunch that he might be able to offer a few suggestions."

Giles was lounging by the parlor fireplace when the doors flew open with a bang. The steward bounded to attention and snapped a salute—but it was only Nathan. Illeinina trotted behind him, and Giles frowned to see the way the prince ignored her; however, judging by the expressions on both faces, perhaps Nathan had an unusual reason for his distraction.

Nathan stopped pacing and confronted his steward.

"How long has my father been tightening his belt?" He demanded.

The question sounded so absurd coming from the happy-go-lucky Prince that Giles almost balked, but he answered truthfully, "Since the last famine, your highness."

"Famine? Ha!" Nathan wagged his head. "I didn't even know there was a famine!" He frowned deep in thought. He dropped into the chair across from Giles. "Is that what a king does when his kingdom is suffering, Giles? Does he take the shortage upon himself?"

Giles could not understand what had worked such a change in the prince. Nathan had never had occasion to ask Giles about kingly behavior—but here it was at last. "It is indeed, my prince," he answered. "They say the mark of a true king is to be first in every battle, last in every retreat, and—when there is hunger—take pleasure in a scantier meal than anyone else in the land."

"And… Is my father a true king, Giles?" Nathan asked.

Giles nodded. "I believe he is, Prince."

Nathan remembered the sad faces and the barrenness, and his mind was made up. "Then I want to do that too."

Giles smiled. "I will inform the kitchen staff of the change."

"Good." Nathan stood as if to walk right back out again, but Giles raised a hand to stop him.

"Your highness, what is to be done with the extra stores that have already been purchased for the meals?"

Nathan waved away the issue. "I don't know; throw it out—"

"Nathan!" Giles hadn't meant for the reaction to come out so sharply, but it was too late to bite his tongue now. Nathan stiffened, but still kept his back to the steward.

Ylaine moved in and placed a hand on Nathan's arm. He glanced at her, and she nodded toward Giles. Reluctantly, he turned back around. "What?"

Giles did not frown, but harbored a look of disapproval in his eyes. "I understand that the food has already been purchased for royal consumption, and if it is not consumed, it will spoil… but throwing it out? Are you sure that is the sort of example you want to set for the other nobles in the kingdom?"

Nathan blinked. "I… I never thought of it that way…" He stammered. Another glance at Illeinina, and she nodded toward Giles a second time. "What would you do with it, Giles?"

The steward rubbed the back of his neck. Perhaps allowing the mysterious girl to remain so close to the prince was having a more profound effect than he anticipated! "Well," he said, glancing at the papers he had been steadily recording notes on over the last few years, "the food has been purchased, so it cannot be returned to the sellers—but, if your lordship is willing, I was thinking it might go well for your reputation if the food was given away freely, to those citizens suffering the most because they cannot afford market prices."

"Giving it away?" Nathan repeated with a startled air. "Hmm, and I suppose it will encourage the people to see their future ruler as benevolent and selfless."

Giles nodded. "It would indeed."

Nathan nodded, "All right, make it so."

Giles couldn't restrain a satisfied grin as he pulled out the paper and pointed to the space at the bottom. "Merely sign this edict and affix your signet, Prince, and the distribution can begin immediately."

Nathan's eyes widened as he noticed for perhaps the first time that there were many such papers waiting on Giles' desk. He dropped the proposed edict and looked at the steward with a suspicious squint. "Just how many of these edicts have you prepared for me?"

Giles shrugged. "Only as many as I believed necessary, highness." *And with all the court sessions slipping unnoticed by the father and son, with the Council assuming more and more control—there have been quite a few!* He thought to himself.

"How long has this been going on?" Nathan flipped through the pile in amazement. "Has my father seen any of these plans?"

Giles sighed and shook his head. "No, highness. You know that your father has not left the castle for some time, and he only listens to the Royal Council—and they will not allow me these propositions, since some of them supersede their own. I am only steward of the castle, and the only one who has heard my counsel is you, Prince Nathan."

Ylaine watched the young prince consider his steward's words. She saw in that moment a reflection of her own life under the water: a King set in his ways and largely ignorant of the goings-on around the kingdom, and a young royal set to inherit a kingdom he knows almost nothing about. Ylaine thought of the advice that Giles gave, and compared it to the advice she had received from Nayidia. Some of what her nurse told her was good—but had Nayidia actually ever told Ylaine about the goodness in her father, the way Giles spoke of King Theodore?

Nathan sighed, calling Ylaine's attention back to the scene at hand.

"Well then," declared the young prince. "You've had my ear in more ways than one, Giles." He grinned as Giles smirked. "So now," Nathan spread the proposals on the desk, "why don't you tell me about all these 'reforms' you've been plotting behind my back?"

Giles looked over at his young charge. "I would be honored, your highness," he said. "May I ask what brought about this change?"

Nathan glanced toward Ylaine and gave a shy half-smile. "I have lived for so long under a father who closed his eyes to hardship, with no one to step forward and show me the things I had become blind to, myself. Today I actually opened my eyes and saw what was really going on around here—thanks to Illeinina."

Ylaine's heart beat at triple speed to hear him say that. Giles' next comment dimmed her hopes somewhat.

"I am glad to hear of it, my prince. I confess I have waited for this moment, never knowing if it would come." He handed the sheaf of papers over to the prince. "I hope you're not expecting these initial reforms to remove the necessity of joining Crossway—it will take a few years for these small changes to be able to sustain the whole kingdom!"

Nathan nodded. "Oh, no; I know this. No, we'll still have to see what Princess Melinda is actually like; maybe she's not half-bad."

Just then, a courier rapped on the door.

"Yes?" Nathan waved him in.

The man bowed low. "Beg pardon," he said, "I have been sent by the harbor master to inform you that the royal schooner from Crossway is nearing the harbor."

Nathan saw that his father had already dressed for the occasion. Giles clapped him on the shoulder.

"No time like the present!" He cried.

Nathan turned and helped Ylaine to her feet. "Come with me," he said, "it will be more fun that way. I bet you've always wanted to meet a real princess up close, haven't you?"

He wondered why she suddenly turned very red and hid her face as they walked.

Chapter 7

Enter The Queen

Ylaine stood very still at Nathan's side as the royal schooner pulled into the harbor. The only people visible on-board were the crew at this point, but she knew the Queen and Princess would be emerging once everything was ready. Ylaine consoled herself with the knowledge that she would not have to wait much longer. She had never had to stand in one place for this long, and her legs were getting tired. Besides, Nathan still had not made any kind of profession of love, and that meant that tomorrow would be her last chance to find out if he really did love her. Did she really want to spend most of her remaining time just standing in one place?

At last, the crewmembers began casting out lines to moor it to the dock, but still they saw no sign of the royal guests. Ylaine let her mind wander—as soon as the guests had been duly escorted to the palace, as etiquette demanded, Nathan had promised they could sneak out and perhaps lunch at the Lake. It would be her first time near the water since she had surfaced. Ylaine quivered with excitement at the thought of just her and Nathan alone, as it was at the beginning. Perhaps then he might...

A loud trumpet fanfare interrupted her thoughts. A page in a frilly collar stood at the top of the gangplank and shouted, "Your Majesties, King Theodore and Prince Nathan, our most distinguished hosts, please may I present to you Queen Devaine and Princess Melinda of Crossway!"

In a fluffy cloud of silk and a resplendence of diamonds, Their Majesties disembarked.

Queen Devaine was indeed a rather plump sort of woman, and not very graceful. She bore herself with unwavering dignity however, and led her daughter right to the dais before the King and Prince.

When she curtsied deeply, King Theodore said, "Your Majesty, thank you for gracing our humble kingdom with your presence."

"It is an honor," Queen Devaine replied, "to count Overcliff among the allies of our fair kingdom." She nudged her daughter forward. "And may I present to you my daughter, Melinda?"

Ylaine felt the hot blood rushing through her suddenly freeze in her veins—she felt as if someone had thrust her back under the water again. Melinda was not just pretty, she was by far the most beautiful human being Ylaine had ever seen. Her clear blue eyes outshone Ylaine's, and her golden hair gleamed brighter than the necklaces she wore. She curtsied as gracefully as a flower waving in the breeze, and said to Nathan, "It is an honor to make your acquaintance."

At the sound of her voice, Ylaine felt her heart tearing just as her tail had when she drank the potion. Not just the simple words Melinda spoke, but the clear, lilting music in them! Ylaine realized then how accustomed she had been to her new, dead voice. Now, hearing the Princess filled her with the longing to forgo it all and jump back into the sea and reclaim her gift from Nayidia, just to hear it again—magic or no magic.

Ylaine felt Nathan release her hand, and he took those of Melinda instead. "Princess Melinda," he said, glancing over his shoulder at Ylaine, "May I present Lady Illeinina: a visitor like yourself, and my dear friend."

His assertion filled Ylaine with warmth once more, and she smiled at Nathan, but he still held Melinda's hand. She nodded curtly to the tormented young woman.

"How delightful!" she trilled again, sending another pang through Ylaine's chest.

Queen Devaine already hung on King Theodore's arm, chatting away animatedly as the king nodded and muttered and tried his best to keep up. Smoothly, Nathan fell into step next to Melinda.

"Shall we?" he invited her.

"Indeed," Melinda murmured coyly, and no one gave Ylaine even a second glance as she stood there upon the dais, alone.

Her vision blurred, and suddenly, Ylaine felt a wetness in her eyes and she could no longer see or breathe easily, as if her gills had opened. She knew they had not, and the water seemed to spring from within her eyes and trickle down her cheeks.

The soft press of fabric on her cheek made her blink, which cleared her vision somewhat. A man stood before her, offering his handkerchief—Giles, the man who had called her Princess. He said nothing as she scrubbed the wetness from her face, only offered his arm as Nathan once had. Ylaine took it, and Giles escorted her to the palace behind the rulers of Crossway and Overcliff.

Inside the castle, the air of formality was nearly palpable. Queen Devaine didn't seem to notice that the front hall servants were also the dining room wait staff as she gushed, "Oh, what a fine palace this is! How so very nice and roomy. A bit empty, but we shall soon fill it with galas aplenty, shall we not, King Theodore?"

The king smiled and nodded, but only Nathan knew from the expression on his father's face that Theodore had not heard a word she said.

The five royals sat to dine and the servants set a single dish before each of them.

As they ate, Miranda suddenly turned to Ylaine.

"So, what kingdom are you from?" She inquired lightly.

Ylaine balked at speaking, for she knew the stuttering that would surely come with it.

Nathan saved her from reply. "We were under the impression that she was from your own kingdom of Crossway," he explained.

"Well, imagine that!" remarked Queen Devaine, picking delicately over the small pheasant on her plate. "Which part, my dear? The Verdant Woods? Or perhaps nearer to—"

"The h-h-harbor t-t-t-town," Ylaine supplied, hoping it was vague enough to fool the queen.

It certainly seemed to satisfy her. "Ah, I see," Devaine returned to polishing off the meal set before her.

Once the plates were empty, nobody missed the glances Their Crossway Majesties were giving to the kitchen door. King Theodore shifted uncomfortably, but Giles cleared his throat, and Nathan's gaze shifted to the steward. A raising of the eyebrows, and a subtle nod told the Prince that now might be a wonderful time to strike up some sort of conversation.

Before he could say a word, Queen Devaine suddenly dropped her fork and asked, "King Theodore, has Overcliff been struck by famine recently?"

The king furrowed his brow at the word *recently*. "The last harvest was a good one; why do you ask?"

Devaine smiled demurely and fingered the necklaces she wore. "I suppose I might be mistaken in assuming that grand feasts are common manners between dignitaries. It is certainly thus on the mainland. Why, even a Baron, when he visits a Lord—"

"We were lucky enough last harvest," Nathan spoke up with an edge in his voice, "but not everyone has always been so fortunate. A hard winter and a bad harvest the year before caused much distress in the outlying towns." He looked keenly at the queen. "In the interest of our citizens, my father and I have grown content with simpler meals, since our gentry would not be much more than a commoner on the mainland." With a smirk he added, "I hope this does not disagree with Your Majesties' digestion."

Giles winced at the Prince's impertinent sarcasm, but the Queen was gracious enough to overlook that comment. "Well," said Devaine, grinning at King Theodore, "let me assure you, once Overcliff and Crossway are united, the King and his son shall dine heartily once again!"

"Just think, mother," agreed Princess Melinda, filling the hall with her melodious voice, "if we were to invite merchants and carnivals here, Overcliff could become a pleasure island and bring not only money but additional residents." She smiled benignly.

Giles grunted, but did not say anything.

Her thoughts screamed desperately as Ylaine fixed her eyes on Nathan, as if she could call his attention and remind him of all they had talked about in the last couple days, all the plans for reform they had made. With Melinda on his other side, there was not much she could do or say that could compete with that ethereal voice. Ylaine slid her hand across the table and brushed her fingers against the back of his hand. He flinched, and subconsciously shifted his hand away, but he addressed Melinda, "Actually, Princess, we do have some reforms ready to enact which will allow the farmers and craftsmen of Overcliff to be better able to produce the wares that will benefit the kingdom, and also receive the most return for their work."

Both women glanced at each other before staring at the Prince with wide eyes.

"Indeed?" The Queen queried slowly. She pursed her exquisite lips. "Do you not think that by empowering the poor you are upsetting the balance of power?"

Nathan squinted in confusion. Giles had never mentioned this. "How so?"

Devaine dabbed delicately at the corners of her mouth. "In Crossway," she explained, "the classes are distinct and obvious and everyone knows their place, therefore we live in harmony and lower classes respect the higher ones. If your reforms are as aggressive as you say they are, you will lose that distinction and throw the kingdom into chaos."

Melinda pushed aside her plate for the servants to collect and joined in the conversation. "Besides, it sounds like a lot of work for just one person." She flashed a glittering smile at Nathan. "I would think a prince as young as you would still be cherishing his time of less obligation." She laid a calculating hand on his shoulder, and he caught the faint scent of something sweet and pleasant as she whispered, "There is no need to play at being King just yet."

Nathan was feeling giddy at the way these ladies spoke. The whole business of being officially royal was still rather new to him, and basically all his information till now had come from Giles—and what did a steward know about being king, anyway? Hearing the Queen and Princess speak so assuredly about regal matters, Nathan found himself inclined to trust their words.

Out of habit, he glanced toward Giles; the expression on that faithful steward's face called to mind all the worthwhile advice he had given the young prince. No amount of purring and petting could quite banish that. Nathan shied away from Melinda only slightly, and spoke with difficulty, "On the contrary, ah, Madam, I am obligated to serve my people, rather than merely be served by them. Leadership and power, erm, are earned—I mean, learned—and, uh, practiced. True leadership is not something that comes on a person all at once, like an illness or some kind of magic spell!"

Melinda giggled, and Nathan experienced the distinct impression that he hadn't clearly said what he meant.

"What charming things you say," gushed the Princess. "If only I could understand them. You speak of power, dear Prince, and yet you don't seem to have much at all, if you don't mind my saying."

The more Nathan watched those mischievous blue eyes, the less he could think straight. "When I am King of Overcliff—"

Melinda cut him off. "Oh, but just think of all the good times we will have in Crossway. We have large meadows for riding horses, our forest stretches on for miles and is just brimming with game, and the carnivals that happen in so many different places absolutely all the time. Can Overcliff offer any of that, such as it is?" She blinked coquettishly.

Nathan finally found the resolve to counter her charms: he resorted to arrogance. He stood and offered his arm to Melinda, a determined light in his eye. "You think we have nothing here?" He snorted. "It just so happens, Princess, that I have had plenty of experience escorting damsels among the diversions of the island."

Melinda smiled and took his arm while the King and Queen watched them. "Indeed?" She queried dubiously.

Nathan grinned and took up her obvious challenge. "Let me show you what Overcliff has to offer!" He stood and offered his arm to her.

The King and Queen stood as well, with Devaine snatching up Theodore's arm, which left Ylaine unaccompanied. She melted into the wall behind her as the foursome swept out of the Great Hall, every bit the regal, human monarchs they were. Not even Nathan gave a second thought for the fair, dark-haired maiden he left behind for this new and shining beauty. Feeling more like an imposter wearing a false skin than ever before, Ylaine vanished to her room and did not emerge for the rest of the night.

৩৫ ৯৯

Giles sighed as he traversed down the hall after everyone had eaten and retired for the night. When would Nathan learn? He had thought the tour would be most successful; indeed, he had never seen the Prince so devoted to kingdom matters as he had been. Then the Queen arrived and he was back to being the old Nathan again.

Only when his guests were safely retired did the young prince remember the one guest to whom he still and would forever owe a debt. Unfortunately, she had taken her leave some time before, so Prince Nathan immediately dispatched Giles to ensure her comfort! Such concern he showed!

Chattering voices caught his attention. Did one of them belong to Lady Illeinina? Giles stopped to listen outside the door.

"Did you see the stables when we came in? Oh, just think of the carriage rides!"

"Frankly, mother, I was more interested in the gardens; so wide and beautiful! Royal life is everything we imagined!"

"You're lucky your Prince still looks young and fresh," the first voice snorted, and with growing consternation Giles deduced he was listening to a rather unmannerly conversation between the Royal ladies of Crossway! "The King is certainly much more withered than the sea witch made him out to be."

"Remember, mother? If I can get the prince to marry me, you won't have to marry the king."

"Good point; you'll have to get him off these *reform* ideas of his, though; no sense in getting altruistic just when we have the chance for ultimate power!"

"Don't worry, Ma; I'll make sure *our* money isn't wasted on the poor, dying peasants of Overcliff."

"That's my girl." The Queen laughed. "Speaking of peasants—if only the ladies of Port-Town could see us now, eh, Meggie?"

"Ma!" Whined the Princess, "stop calling me that! You've got to remember I am Melinda now. Though," she broke off with a giggle, "I was more thinking of what Lord Jamison might think of his laundress hob-nobbing with the King!"

Both women dissolved into giggles. Giles had heard enough. He burst into the room, red with wrath.

"Impostors!" He seethed, "Traitors!"

Devaine and Meggie rose to their feet in alarm as Giles stepped among them.

"How dare you!" Devaine began, but Giles stopped her.

"I know what you are!" He cried. "You are in no way the royalty you claim to be, and certainly it will come before the king at once!" He turned to march straight back to the King's hall.

A gust of wind rushed through the room and slammed the door in front of his face.

Devaine sauntered up behind him. "You see?" She taunted him. "You are only a servant. The true power is with us." She smiled sweetly at him, her eyes glinting cruelly. "And if you dare interfere with our plans for Overcliff," her eyes narrowed. "I will convince King Theodore to have you executed on the spot. Do we have an understanding?"

Giles could not tear his eyes away from the door before him. He found he lacked the willpower to open it again, leaving him at her mercy—what had she done? How could one woman have the wherewithal to pull off such a fantastic charade? Pretending to be the queen—what did she mean by "power"? Had she called up the wind somehow? His jaw clenched as he stared at the brazen woman. He nodded at the widow.

"Do you really think a parlor trick such as *that* will prevent honest hearts from discovering the *truth* about you?" He seethed.

Devaine's face twisted into a horrible scowl and she struck Giles across the mouth. "Listen to me, *steward*," she hissed, "you are meddling in powers you do not understand—and, think what you like, no amount of 'honest hearts' will ever convince a ruler to trust the word of a *servant* over that of a Queen." She leaned in close as the breeze behind her swirled around the room with an ominous roar. "And if you *ever* speak a word of this in the presence of the King, I will kill Prince Nathan." Her eyes glinted madly, and Giles felt cold horror twist in his heart at the black emptiness of her gaze. "Have I made myself clear?" She whispered.

Giles kept his face impassive, but he couldn't meet those dead, wicked eyes. "Perfectly," he replied.

Devaine did not waver. Pulling his chin so that he was forced to look down at her, she prompted, "Perfectly, what?"

"Perfectly.... Your Majesty." The words tasted like bile on his tongue.

She nodded. "That's better. You may go."

Another wind swept around him and carried Giles out the door and closed it behind him.

Chapter 8

Exposed

Ylaine awoke cautiously the next morning. Today marked the last of the three days, and she had no idea how quickly the potion's effects would subside. A careful inspection in the mirror yielded nothing concerning. Of course, Melinda's presence did complicate things, but Ylaine firmly believed that Nathan did indeed prefer her company over anyone else. She had spent all night convincing herself that his behavior at the harbor the previous evening had merely been for show.

She selected a dress—rosebuds on a white field, with a wide red sash—and prepared to convene in the great hall for breakfast. Perhaps, if she was lucky, she would meet Nathan coming from his room in the opposite wing.

Sure enough, when she reached the top of the stairs, he had only gone as far as the first landing. Ylaine gave a little cough in her throat, the way Giles did when he wanted to get Nathan's attention without using his words.

It worked. The way Nathan turned to face her, and then froze in place as she descended toward him, made her heart beat rapidly again. She knew that, even if she were to become a Mermaid after today, she would remember the smile that burst on his face for the rest of her life.

She opened her mouth, and "Good morning, Nathan" was on her tongue—

Then a clear voice sang out, "Good morning, Prince!"

Ylaine gripped the banister as Princess Melinda sailed down the stairs and attached herself to Nathan's arm. He smiled at the flaxen-haired beauty as she continued jabbering.

"Did you sleep well last night? I know I never had a better night's sleep in another country. Oh, I am so glad to be here in Overcliff. How delightful the castle is, and the sound of the sea was so soothing." She drew a long sigh through her petite nose. "I feel so refreshed. I hope today we can have a tour of the kingdom. This palace is certainly much nicer than any other castle we've ever visited."

They disappeared around the corner, and Ylaine struggled to keep up as the stinging water confounded her vision yet again. She gulped a breath of air and fought to hold it, trying to calm her unsteadiness and retain her composure.

She had one hope she clung to: she was still human. If Nathan truly had loved her for those first two days, perhaps she still had three days from this point to hear him declare as much–but at the rate Melinda leaned on his shoulder and whispered sweet nothings in his ear and babbled on about anything and everything, he could not get a word in edgewise, much less a moment alone with Ylaine.

By the time she arrived in the Great Hall, Devaine and Melinda already entertained their hosts with incredible tales from the mainland. While they talked, Ylaine glanced around the room. There was the door that led to the parlor where all the drafts of the Prince's reform plans sat idly by, waiting for the young man to put them into action. Maybe, if she could just drop a hint of something—Ylaine glanced at Melinda, deep in some hilarious anecdote about a fox hunt; Ylaine had no inkling of what a fox might look like, though she had seen the Mermen go out hunting in the deep black sea plenty of times.

She sighed; it was hopeless.

Her attention turned to Giles. Normally he watched Nathan with a smiling countenance. This morning he stood straight as a ship's mast, a frown plastered over his face, and his eyes fixed on the King. A few times

Ylaine saw him glance at her, but she had no idea why. The voices of the Royal ladies of Crossway filled the air, but Ylaine struggled with a tension she could not fathom. She had not quite finished her portion but she slipped away from the table; everyone was so busy talking that no one seemed to notice her departure.

She wandered into the corridors, enjoying the blessed silence—but not ten minutes later, the Queen's hearty laugh grated on her ears. Ylaine traveled down the hall toward the inner courtyard, but very soon, Nathan and Melinda staggered into the area, practically falling over each other with amusement. Her heart began to climb into her throat; Ylaine was having trouble breathing again. In desperation, she flew down the hall and into the small study. Faint wafts of music touched her ears, accompanying a high, lilting voice. She did not even know that Nathan enjoyed such music—not that she could ever make it, not without her gift like this. Groaning as if her body would burst, Ylaine wrapped her arms over her head to shut out all sound.

She did not know how long she remained there, but when she finally picked up her head, all was silent. Ylaine slipped out into the hall. What were they doing now?

She heard rustling papers as she walked by the parlor. Was Nathan showing Melinda his plans, after all? She peeked in the doorway.

Giles sat alone among the papers. Ylaine nearly decided to move on and find Nathan, but just then, Giles sensed her presence and whirled around.

"Oh," he grunted. "It's just you, Milady. I thought you had gone with the Prince and Princess."

Ylaine entered the room, and Giles stood to offer her his chair.

"I d-did not kn-n-know they had g-gone anywhere," she stammered.

Giles shrugged. "It is only a horse ride on this very small island; they will no doubt be back by the evening meal."

Ylaine gestured to the desk. "M-meanwhile, you d-d-do his w-work?"

Giles leaned over and placed both hands on the desk with a groan. "Apparently this princess and the Queen have convinced him that the negotiations with Crossway would be more important than reforming Overcliff, and if the two will become one kingdom, where would be the point in improving anything ourselves?" Giles scowled darkly at the papers, but Ylaine sensed there was more than just the forgotten plans on the steward's mind.

"Wh-what t-t-troubles you?" She asked.

Giles blinked, "Hm? What? Oh, it—it's nothing." He pushed away from the table and faced the window. At last, he sighed.

"Illeinina," he said, striding back toward her, "I must tell you of a scheme so powerful that I can do nothing against it—but at the same time I must tell someone, with the hope that they can do what I cannot."

Ylaine felt her pulse quicken. "What scheme?"

Giles bent in close and whispered, "The Queen and Princess are not who they say they are. I overheard them last night, talking of how they were going to force the prince into marriage and force the king to give up the kingdom—but the truth is that they are only servants in a Lord's house on Crossway."

Ylaine's mind reeled; servants! And this whole time she had envied Melinda as someone more eligible to marry the Prince, when really she was just as much an impostor as Ylaine herself!

"H-how?" She gasped. "How could they do this?"

Giles wagged his head. "Some devilry at work. I heard the false Queen mention the assistance of a sea witch—but such a thing must surely be impossible, mustn't it?"

Sea witch! Ylaine's heart jumped into her throat; the only one in the castle with ties to the sea would be her. Had some nefarious enemy from Undersea discovered her desertion and now her presence in Overcliff made her unwitting hosts a target? "What can we do?" She asked.

Giles stood with agony in his face. "I wish I knew! The Queen has threatened me that if anyone dares interfere with their plans... She will kill Prince Nathan."

"NO!" Ylaine could not help herself, she leaped to her feet so quickly, she almost lost her balance and fell over.

Giles supported her till she could steady herself. "Milady, please! There are no dictates of decorum ingrained in these women, I know they will not hesitate to get what they want. We must think of some way to warn Nathan without them knowing, but until then, we must agree to give them no sign that—"

"Hush!" Ylaine's quick ears caught the sound of a footfall in the hall.

Giles caught himself and he began speaking loudly.

"My dear girl, if you want to get the Prince's attention at all, you must do these exercises we have discussed to be rid of that despicable stutter! He won't look at you twice as long as you have it."

He glanced toward the doorway. Sure enough, Queen Devaine stood just outside, staring keenly at the two of them.

Giles nodded for Ylaine to continue the ruse.

"Th-thank you G-g-Giles," she said as distinctly as she could.

He gave a loud, theatrical groan. "Ugh! You are not even trying! The prince as good as belongs to Melinda at the rate you're going! Go run along, practice what I have told you."

Ylaine walked toward the door. When she opened it, Devaine was gone, but she caught sight of a rotund bustle just disappearing around the corner. She went straight back to her room, with its window overlooking the stables. She could see the coastline from here.

A sea witch! The last sea witch Ylaine had ever heard of was a haggard old crone who invaded a Council meeting when she was only a little fry. She remembered the pale-grey, withered Mermaid shrieking at King Davor because he had dismissed her son Gondu from the Royal Guard for cowardice in battle. Was the witch still alive? Was this her way of getting revenge on Ylaine's father?

Nathan and Melinda did not return till after nightfall, and Ylaine slept fitfully, dreaming of the sea witch and the two impostors either murdering Nathan or killing her.

The next morning, Ylaine awoke with a heavy yawn and a sigh. When she stretched her mouth and gasped, she heard a slight popping sound. She stopped; what had popped? Something in her throat? She breathed again. Something fluttered. Suddenly, it seemed that Ylaine could not get as much breath as usual, that she had to gasp several times to get the amount of air in one breath. Then she knew what happened: her gills were coming loose. The potion was slowly wearing off from the inside, because she had failed to secure her true love.

Ylaine tried to continue as if nothing was wrong, dining with the royals as normal. She noticed that the King and Queen talked more openly about uniting the two kingdoms, while Nathan ignored them to wait on Melinda. Ylaine felt that as long as she hid the sound of her furious, shallow panting, she could find a way to reverse this process.

As they dined that afternoon, Melinda turned her sapphire gaze upon the poor lady.

"My dear," she warbled, "Are you well?" The princess grasped Ylaine's hand out of apparent concern. As quickly as she grabbed, she released. "Oh my! Your hands, they feel so cold, like a fish!"

Ylaine looked at her hand in alarm. Was it her imagination, or was her human skin beginning to flake off, revealing the scales underneath?

The breathing difficulty increased. Ylaine knew that she had only a short time to regain the prince's attention. She could not do that while Melinda clung to him like a leech.

"Nathan..." she began, but she could not think of anything to tell him that would send a clear enough message to him without alerting the princess. Ylaine stood and left the room. On her way out, she heard the princess speaking to Nathan.

"She looks so very unwell! I do hope it's not serious. No matter! Dear Prince, you have a lovely green out behind the castle. Do you, perchance, play croquet?"

Ylaine ran to her room. Water! She needed water to saturate her throat. Her gills were not all open because her throat was too dry, but her lungs were no longer processing air as well as a human's did. She found the washbasin and the jug of water. Speedily, she poured the whole jug in and dunked her face.

Relief at last. Ylaine gasped and spluttered as her gills flapped open at the presence of water, and she could breathe normally again.

Suddenly, a pair of hands grabbed her by the shoulders and hauled her out. Ylaine coughed and spluttered as she looked into the horrified face of Giles.

"My lady, have you gone mad?" he demanded forcefully. "What is the meaning of this?"

Ylaine began panting again, and her knees felt weak. She looked down. Her wet human skin sloughed off at an even greater rate. She had no choice but to tell the truth right now, or she would die.

"Giles!" She panted. "You... must... know... the... truth... I... am... not... the... lady... you... think... I... am." She held up her hand for him to see. He held it in his own and studied the revealed scales in surprise as Ylaine continued. "I am... m-Mermaid... traded... voice... to become human... to find... man... I love; the... spell... wearing off... soon I... will be... Mermaid again...and...die...unless I can... win him!"

Giles dropped her hand. "Lady Illeinina—"

She smiled ruefully and shook her head. "I am... Princess Ylaine... of Undersea."

"Your Highness, then," Giles insisted. "To me and to every other human you are none other than the Prince's savior. He owes you his life, we owe you our prince." He rested his fingertips against her chin and tipped her face up. "No more, no less," he assured her. "Therefore I will do everything in my power to provide whatever you need." To demonstrate, he turned and called a passing servant. "Hello, there!"

A maid stuck her head in. "Yes sir?"

"Ask no questions, but only draw a large bath for the lady. Take care it is not too warm."

The orders confused the maid, but Giles had said not to ask questions, so she complied.

Giles assisted Ylaine to the bed. "There is talk of attending the carnival tomorrow, but I will try to speak with Nathan this evening. Rest now, Highness."

The maid left, and Ylaine eagerly slipped into the water. She gulped deeply, feeling the water lift her gills and breath re-energize her whole body. When she emerged a few hours later, she checked her skin carefully. Luckily, only her throat and lungs seemed the most affected; from the outside, only her hands showed any scales. A pair of gloves covered them, and Ylaine could be human once more. She sat before the large hearth as the sun set. She heard a knock at the door.

Queen Devaine stood outside, bearing a tray with two covered platters and two goblets of spiced wine. Her expression was all sympathy and concern.

"I heard you weren't feeling well," she said, coming in and setting the tray on the table, "so I thought you might appreciate some supper with a friend."

Ylaine stared at the plate. She was very hungry, and the wine smelled good. She had thought that Princess Melinda and Queen Devaine viewed her as a threat, but perhaps the whole plot had been the workings of the princess alone. She sat down and supped with the Queen, feeling the stress of the day ebb from her body. She ate the food and drained the goblet; she had never known drink to taste this good. There was a hint of the sea about it...

Ylaine's head dropped, and she slumbered deeply. Devaine smiled as she stood and glanced toward the window.

"Madame Nayidia, you were right," she mused aloud. "The minx is not human after all."

A breezy reply wafted on the wind. *"No sea creature can resist the taste of jetsam-weed. You have done well, Devaine. Soon Overcliff will be yours."*

Devaine smirked at the unconscious victim. "Sleep well, little Mermaid." She extinguished the lights and closed the door.

Chapter 9

The Exchange

Ylaine knew nothing but murky darkness until a voice called her out of the depths.

"Milady! Lady Ylaine! Highness! Wake up!"

Ylaine blinked. Giles stood over her, desperate to awaken her. The sun shone brightly through the window. Why was he so worried? Ylaine felt her hands; why was she wearing gloves? She moved to take them off—then stopped in horror as her skin began to come away with them! Suddenly everything that happened the previous day came back to her in a rush, and she gave such a gasp that her dry gills crackled. She looked up at Giles and tried to ask him for water to moisten her throat, but it was so dry, no sound could pass her lips.

"Wa....wa—wa—" she panted.

The faithful servant understood. He grabbed the fresh jug from the maid and handed it to her. Ylaine gratefully filled her lungs with the liquid.

"Must get...to Nathan!" she cried, pulling her heavy body out of bed. Instead of standing, she collapsed on the floor. Her legs were as limp as fish tails. Giles dove forward and supported her weak body.

"I am afraid you are too late, your highness," he mourned, "The others have already left for the carnival. There will be no hope of finding them now."

Ylaine looked mournfully at her hands. "That's not...the worst..." She offered Giles a hand. Already, the glove hung from it, half-off, revealing the scaled, webbed appendage underneath. She met eyes with the astonished steward.

"I must...get to water... soon!"

Giles immediately gripped the wet, fishy hand in his own dry, firm one.

"Come with me, your Highness."

෴

An hour later, the prince's servant hurried down the lane toward the place where the forest met the edge of the island.

"Nearly there, your Highness!" Giles whispered to the barrow full of burlap sacks.

Ylaine lay tucked inside, with the sacks saturated so she could at least breathe the moist air. In this manner he brought her all the way to a small cove enclosed in the hanging branches of a weeping willow.

"We have arrived, princess," he told her, pulling off the bags to expose her face.

"Leave me here," she instructed. "Wait outside."

Giles hesitated. "Are you sure?" he asked.

Ylaine nodded, "Go now." She didn't want him to see how terribly desperate she had become.

The minute Giles withdrew, Ylaine practically threw herself out of the barrow and to the water's edge. Her gills flared open wide as she gulped the life-giving water. Her arms lost their skin entirely as she reached into the folds of her dress for the mier she had hidden there. Ylaine placed the smooth, round shell against the bank, where it attached with a slurping sound. Desperately, Ylaine struck it as hard as she could and the shell broke open. She could not hear the sound above the water, but, as promised, the lean form of Nayidia appeared just under the surface within moments. Ylaine dipped her face into the water to speak with her.

"Kelpling!" Nayidia smiled. "How are you? Did you find the human you were looking for? Have you come to reclaim your gift?"

"Yes, I found him, but—oh Nayidia! I need more time!"

"More time?" Nayidia examined the young face above her. "What do you mean? Doesn't he love you?"

Ylaine's chin trembled. "Never mind, there isn't time to explain," she muttered. "Do you still have my gift?"

"Your fairy gift?" Nayidia gestured to the green stone hanging around her neck. "I have it right here. Would you like it back?"

Perhaps if she could sing to Nathan, make him wise enough to see what the Princess was doing, perhaps that would solve everything. "Yes!" She cried.

"Very well," said Nayidia, coyly playing with her braids. "But it's not going to be for free."

Ylaine forced her thoughts away from Nathan to focus on what her godmother had just said. "But Nayidia," she spluttered. "You said that if I wanted it—"

"That was if you had secured the human's love and thus would remain human forever, wasn't it?" Nayidia reminded her. "Anybody can see that's not the case, Kelpling." She pointed as a flap of human skin from Ylaine's cheek broke free and floated away in the water.

Ylaine fought the urge to pull out of the water. Drying wouldn't save her skin now.

Nayidia sighed. "There is something I must tell you, Kelpling—it concerns your father."

Ylaine felt her human heart suddenly threaten to beat its way out of her chest. "Is... Is he unwell?" She gasped.

Nayidia shook her head. "No! Well, at least, not in body; but very much in spirit." She stared directly into Ylaine's eyes as she continued. "When he discovered your absence, he tried to put a bold face on it, saying it was a fate you brought on yourself. But after a while, he began to change. Ylaine," Nayidia reached up to grasp the young princess' hand. "Now I see how much your songs truly meant to him. He has become angry and unpredictable, with a lust for violence against the land-dwellers who have taken away everything he holds dear."

"But they didn't!" Ylaine cried, her heart lurching and her head swirling at the idea. "They didn't take me away!"

"Prove it, then!" Nayidia drew back sharply and folded her arms. "Come back with me, and tell your father what you have discovered. Isn't that what you intended to do?"

Poor Ylaine hardly knew what to think. What she had discovered was a human worthy of her love—and he was in the thrall of two impostors.

"I... I can't!" She cried. "Nayidia, please! There is something very important happening here that will have consequences for both realms. I need to be human, if only for just a little while longer!"

"But if there is a war," Nayidia countered, "won't that affect both realms as well?"

"It will be a while yet before my father figures out how to unite the Merfolk and attack the humans without leaving the water. But here, Nayidia," Ylaine's tone grew more desperate, "here, the prince is facing destruction from one of his own kind! I must save him!"

Nayidia swam in a figure-eight as she pondered deeply how best to help the princess.

"I propose a new bargain," the Mermaid said finally. "Pendant for pendant: I give you the stone with your gift, and you," she pointed to the space beneath Ylaine's chin, "give me the golden shell."

Ylaine's hand flew to the article in question. "What? But Nayidia, that is my birthright!"

Nayidia nodded. "I understand, but trust me, little one! With the pendant, I could prove that you are alive and well, and your father just might listen to me in your place." Nayidia paused to absently pick at one of her braids. "Besides, it won't do you much good if you're going to remain human!" She fixed Ylaine with those clear, icy-blue eyes. "That is what you want, isn't it?"

Ylaine fought within herself; she had kept the necklace as a reminder of her other kingdom—but she would still remember the sea without it, wouldn't she? Certainly giving it up would mean giving up being a Mermaid altogether—but if Nathan really did love her, and if being human meant saving both their kingdoms, did that not matter more than being accepted into the Mer-community?

She unclasped the golden cowrie. "Very well," she sighed.

Nayidia smiled sympathetically as she handed the green stone to Ylaine. "I know how hard this must be for you, Kelpling—you must truly believe in the cause of the land-dwellers."

"I believe in a cause driven by love, not anger," Ylaine affirmed. She prepared to return to attempting to breathe air again. "Thank you, Nayidia—"

"Wait." The Mermaid seemed to consider something deeply. "Before you go, I want to give you something." She reached into the pouch about her waist and pulled out a small vial.

"More potion?" An irrational hope welled in Ylaine's chest.

"Yes; it's some of the one-day potion I had brewing for your birthday. I know it's not much, but—"

Ylaine snatched it up when Nayidia held it out to her. "Oh, thank you, Nayidia."

The Mermaid smiled. "It is the least I can do for my Kelpling. If this works, I suppose I shan't ever see you again."

Ylaine smiled at her dear friend. "With my gift, I can always call you, Nayidia."

Nayidia popped her gills dubiously. "We shall see," she said, and took her leave.

Ylaine pulled her face out of the water and instantly felt short of breath again. She almost could not uncork the vial and drink some, but she managed a portion of the dose.

The effect was both sudden and familiar. Her gills seared over again, and her muscles tightened. In seconds, she no longer felt like she was melting. Ylaine replaced the cork and looked at the green stone hanging from the chain. The gift flashed gold streaks within it. She fastened the chain around her neck, and the moment she did, the stone glowed with an icy intensity, and she felt her lungs and throat expanding to welcome the fairy gift back into their midst. Ylaine took a deep breath, and as she listened to the resonance of the tree, the grass, and the water around her. In fact, she fancied she could even hear the music of the carnival—

The carnival! Ylaine scrambled to her feet and back out into the open.

"Giles!" She called—and nearly laughed to hear the old ring in her voice once more. Oh, how she had missed that!

He appeared, looking very shocked and puzzled. "Your Highness?"

Ylaine guessed that he was probably wondering at not only her voice but also how she had managed to rejuvenate her entire appearance.

"We must get to the Carnival," said Ylaine. "We need to find Nathan!"

Giles' face showed despair as they made their way down the path. "No doubt the Princess intends to make it impossible to find him at all in the noise and crowd."

Ylaine's heart sank as she observed the milling throng just ahead. They would never find him in time with just looking—there had to be a way! They attempted a foray into the crowd, but Ylaine found the mass of faces and bodies confusing to her, and the movement made her unsteady on her feet. She gripped Giles' arm.

"Giles, is there a hill nearby?" she asked.

He skirted a carousing pair and nearly tripped over a punch-drunk old man passed out on the ground. "A hill, ma'am?" he repeated dully.

Ylaine started scanning the terrain herself. "Yes! I need to sing for Nathan!" she replied absently.

Giles was willing to help her—but what could the two have possibly to do with each other. "As I told you before, I don't think—"

"There!" Ylaine pointed to a small knoll just across the way, on the very edge of the party field. "Just get me there!"

Chapter 10

The Carnival

Melinda enjoyed the time of her life at the carnival with Nathan. Who could have guessed that a simple serving woman's daughter could be taken for a princess and captivate the Prince so! It started with the message in a bottle from the most powerful sea witch herself, and then—before one could say *I'm a codfish!*—she was dressing in fine clothes and eating rich foods and cavorting with the Prince! Melinda silently thanked the fates that the sea witch had chosen her, while at the same time she chafed at the strange requirements Madame Nayidia placed on her: "Flatter the Prince, but don't behave as if you know you are his beloved. Cling to him too much, and everyone will know you are a charlatan. You're a princess now; behave like everything is yours for the taking, but under no circumstances should you ever dream of actually taking it!"

Duly noting the sea witch's advice, Melinda laid her golden head lovingly upon the Prince's shoulder and gushed, "Ah! How wonderful you are! I think whoever you choose for your bride will be lucky to have the strongest, kindest, most generous man in the whole world!" They passed by several enticing games and shows. They had been wandering the carnival for hours, but she dare not let the fatigue show.

The Prince didn't seem interested in the carnival any more. He turned his head and looked at Melinda with a strange expression on his face. She drew back somewhat; was it suspicion? Had she gone too far?

"Do you hear that?" he blurted.

The question was so wholly unexpected that it took several seconds for Melinda to comprehend it. "Hear what?" She responded tentatively.

He was adamant now; there was something stirring him like nothing else had all evening. "Listen! That music!" He cried.

Melinda couldn't hear a thing over the clamor of multiple minstrel bands playing different tunes at different times, and the chatter of the people. She tried to hold onto his arm. "Nathan I don't know—"

"Ylaine." The haunting melody reached his ear, placing in his mind the image of the girl he had known as Illeinina, but somehow the name was just a little bit different. As the tones seeped deeper, seemed to penetrate his very heart with understanding, Nathan looked at Melinda and recognized instantly what she truly was: a coarse country maid. The ravishing beauty melted away, and left a dull, pasty girl in its place, clinging to his arm and staring at him with hungry eyes. He grimaced.

Meanwhile, the strange name and the way he looked at her sent Melinda into a panic. "Who?" She squeaked.

Nathan dropped Melinda's arm for the first time that day and actually began walking away from her. He called over his shoulder,

"Her name is Ylaine, and I've got to find her!"

ﾟᦅᦆ ᦆᦅﾟ

Ylaine closed her eyes as she sang, shutting out the world. There was no one but her and Nathan; no more conniving father, no more simpering princess, no more false queen pretending to be her friend and then drugging her to try and remove all hope of her ever achieving her dream. All that melted away and disappeared as she sang,

"Hear my song, Prince of my heart!
Pride, forbear, and vanity, depart!
See the truth, in her shining glory,
Come near to me, and hear my story!"

She gasped as suddenly his arms enfolded her, and he held her close, whispering over and over in her ear,

"Ylaine… Ylaine…. Ylaine!"

"Yes," she whispered back, "My name is Ylaine, and I love you more than life itself." It felt so freeing to be able to tell him how she felt! Perhaps now Melinda's spell was broken, and she could tell him of the deception. "Nathan, you have to listen to me; Queen Devaine and Princess Melinda are not who they say they are! They are only impersonating royalty; this was all a plot by an evil Mermaid—a sea witch—to gain control of Overcliff and the water around it!"

Nathan pulled away in shock at the news. "What?" he gasped. "What are you even talking about?"

"Well, well!" A harsh voice cut the air behind her. "The Sleeping Beauty has awakened, and such wild tales she has to tell!"

Ylaine turned to face Devaine, while Melinda lunged for Nathan and pulled him away.

"Admit it!" The young woman snapped. "You aren't really the Queen of Crossway! I bet the true rulers do not even know that you are here!"

Devaine blinked in surprise, and Ylaine thought she had scored a hit.

"Do my ears deceive me?" Devaine gasped loudly. "Is this not Lady Illeinina, the stuttering half-wit under the Prince's generous patronage?" She looked around, and people nodded under her gaze. Devaine returned her eyes to the quivering girl before her. "How is it that she speaks so clearly now, when she is spouting such atrocious things about her fellow guests? Could it be, my dear, that you are not what you would appear?" She arched her eyebrows smugly.

"How dare you!"

The cry rang out from somewhere within the throng. People parted as Giles worked his way to the center of the crowd. He jabbed a finger at Devaine while she glared at him in cold fury. "How dare you question the honor of the one who saved the Prince's life!"

"Be silent, steward!" Devaine spat. "Yes, I have heard the romantic tale—but it seems no one but my dear daughter has ever thought to consider the motive behind the rescue! Dear Prince," she turned back to Nathan, "are you aware of a second domain within the boundaries of Overcliff?"

Nathan blinked, as Melinda wrapped both arms around his shoulder. "Second domain?" He queried.

"Yes," Devaine smiled coldly. "That of... Mermaids."

A chuckle rippled through the crowd. King Theodore stepped forward. "Milady," he said to her, "you are mistaken; there have not been any Mermaids in existence since my father was a very young boy."

Nathan stared at his father; he had never known Mermaids existed at all!

But Devaine was nodding, and Ylaine trembled at her intentions. "Ah, there you are mistaken, my Lord, for they are very much alive, and as numerous as they are strong—and there is one in your very midst!"

A gasp went up from the now-silent carnival. Everyone looked to his neighbor and under nearby crates and rent flaps.

The King drew himself up sharply, his face black as a thundercloud. "What is the meaning of this?" He demanded of Devaine.

The wily woman turned and plucked a pitcher of water from the hands of a woman standing behind her. Before anyone could move, she flung the contents of the pitcher right over Ylaine's head.

At first, several people reproached the woman for acting so crazily, but just then Melinda screeched, "Oh my! Look at her face!"

Ylaine lifted her hands to her cheeks. The potion was wearing off faster this time; the skin was already peeling away. Not even a declaration of love this very instant could save her now. "No!" She gasped.

Devaine was addressing the crowd. "Here is your little heroine! Here is the one who saved your prince! Did no one stop to think what business a young woman had to be swimming during a storm? Of course she saved him—she probably caused the storm in the first place!"

"That is not true!" Ylaine insisted, but the skin had already begun to slide off her shoulders, revealing her blue scales underneath.

"Merciful heavens," spluttered the King, "Devaine, what have you done to her?"

"Only exposed her true form, Theodore," Devaine explained earnestly. "She is a Mermaid, who has taken human form to seduce the Prince—"

"She is a princess!" Giles insisted. "Her father is a king, she is no less noble than the Prince himself! Unlike y—"

Devaine cut him off. "Well, isn't that just fascinating! The King of the Merfolk sends his own daughter up to masquerade as a human? Why would he do that? Is it because he wanted her to spy on this human kingdom, to see if there are any souls worth enslaving when they rise up and bring the entire kingdom under the sea?"

"What?" Nathan cried.

Ylaine tried to speak, but the skin slipped off her nose and covered her mouth. Her gills were beginning to loosen at the presence of water in her throat.

Devaine was not finished. "Surely you cannot think that a union between a Mermaid and a human would ever be considered—and what better excuse to declare war than to accuse King Theodore of kidnapping the Mer-king's daughter?"

"What?" roared the King.

Ylaine gasped to shout, "That's not true!" But her gills suddenly snapped open and she choked on the dry air.

Devaine gazed at her pityingly. "You didn't really expect us to believe you came of your own accord, did you, little fish-girl? That you came for—what was it—love?" She snorted.

Ylaine felt her knees buckle, and she fought to stay upright. "I... Did... Come... For.... Love..." She rasped, gasping furiously for each word.

"Oh, poppycock," Devaine waved a hand. "Even the Prince knows that you did not stand a chance of getting his attention without your magic voice!"

Ylaine struggled to think through the fog in her mind; what did Devaine know about her gift? She turned to look at Nathan, even as the skin from her cheek slid down her neck. "Nathan?" She whispered. "I swear, I did not deceive or enchant you—"

"But you did." He stared straight at her, unblinking. "What the Queen says is true; I harbored no thought for you, no love in my heart—until I heard you singing!"

Her heart ripped yet again. No love? Then why had the magic potion lasted as long as it did? Had she been fooling herself this whole time? "Please! I was just—"

"Trying to seduce him," Devaine finished for her. "Yes, we know. But your little plot failed! Go on back to the water, little fish!" She snarled. "There's no one here on land for you!"

Tears slipped down Ylaine's face for the second time, and quite possibly the last.

"Nathan?" she begged.

He would not respond. Desolate, Ylaine ran from the

crowd—who gave her wide clearance to pass through them—and away from the carnival, down to the sea.

There was a moment of uneasy tension, then the crowd began to edge away slowly. No one was much interested in the carnival diversions, but nobody wanted to stand around staring at the fight that was no longer happening. Melinda gave the arm she clutched a little squeeze.

"Well," she sighed, "I am so glad that little hussy is gone! Now that's over, Your—" She stopped.

Giles and not Nathan grinned down at her.

Melinda pulled a face and pushed the serving-man away from her. "Eww!" she cried. "Where's Nathan? Where did he go? Nathan!" She ran around the carnival as the swelling noise drowned out her squeaky voice. "NATHAN!"

The prince had vanished.

Chapter 11

Truth Will Out

Ylaine rushed blindly to the edge of the land. She felt the hard dirt turn into sand under her feet. Her toe caught on a protruding tree root and she sprawled on the ground and her hand struck water. Sobs shook her body and she curled her legs close to herself.

"Nayidia!" She called. Her gift added overtones to her voice. She raised her head and cried again, "Nayidia!"

Her godmother appeared in the water before her. There might have been anger in her eyes, but the water obscured them just enough.

Her voice was cloying as she soothed, "My dear Kelpling, why are you crying?"

Ylaine uncurled and let her feet dip into the water. "It's no use!" She wept. "I don't want to be human anymore!"

Nayidia swam in slow rotations, keeping her eyes fixed on Ylaine's face. "But Ylaine, don't you remember? I hold the golden cowrie; if you return, I will be the Royal and the only way you could live in Undersea would be as my servant." She paused to let her words sink in. "Is this really what you want?" Her eyes were wide and innocent, but the implications of the choice pressed in on Ylaine's mind.

She gave a shaky sigh. "Yes; there is nothing—"

"Ylaine?" The sound of her name stopped the words in her throat. "Ylaine, wait!"

Ylaine whirled around to behold Nathan cresting the hill behind her. He ran down the bank. She saw him draw up short at the sight of the deep-blue-skinned woman just under the surface of the water.

"That's—" he stammered, stumbling back a few paces, "she's a—" he gaped at Ylaine. "You mean it's true?"

Ylaine wanted to pull her feet out of the water, but she could see the scales already forming on her legs. She was trapped there, hovering on the edge of the water.

"Nathan," she gasped, "what are you doing here?"

It took a moment for Nathan to tear his eyes away, but he placed a hand on Ylaine's shoulder.

"Ylaine, Giles told me everything; please don't do this!"

Ylaine opened and closed her mouth a few times before she could find the words. "But… back at the carnival… You said—"

"Only what Devaine wanted to hear," Nathan confirmed. "That way she wouldn't notice when I slipped

away to find you. Please believe me when I say that
I really do love you!" he begged.

A splash made them turn. Ylaine watched in amazement as Nayidia suddenly rose out of the water, encased
in a constant, flowing stream that kept her scales and
gills moist. Fear washed over her as she realized that
Nayidia held the key to the last obstacle that had pre-
vented King Davor from striking sooner—the ability
for a Merperson to leave the water without drying out.

Nayidia pointed an imperious finger at Nathan. "If
you truly love her so much," she demanded, "Then why,
if you were so bold in your love, does she come here
convinced that you do not care for her?" She laughed
mirthlessly. "No, little prince, it is too late. The bargain
has been struck—"

Ylaine could not understand how her godmother
could suddenly turn on her like this. How could the
same Merwoman turn from granting her every wish
to exulting in such cruelty as one seeking vengeance?

While these questions thundered through Ylaine's
mind, Nathan spoke, "Then let me pay it."

Nayidia tipped her head so that a braid slapped the
water. "What?"

Ylaine could not believe what she was hearing.
"Nathan, no!"

He ignored her and continued. "Whatever she has
promised you, take it from me instead. As you said,

the fact that she is here having done all she could and failed is because of me. I am the one who failed, not she." His voice wavered, and he sounded less forceful when he said, "I should be the one to pay."

Nayidia fixed him with her gaze as her tail flipped back and forth. "Are you quite sure?" She asked slowly.

Nathan looked down at Ylaine's horrified face and replied, "As surely as I love her, yes."

Ylaine felt her heart sink within her, even as the skin once hanging from her shoulders and legs at once reformed and she was fully human again.

Nayidia laughed. "Oh, if only you had said that sooner—" she crowed, "but advantages must be taken." She raised her hands and uttered a spell, and in that moment, as the cloud of magic swirled around her, Ylaine saw Nayidia's appearance change. Her skin faded more grey, and her arms shrank within the skin. Her braids folded back and separated into a cloud of white hair—and Ylaine saw her for what she truly was, but too late. Nayidia's spell struck Nathan in the chest and he doubled over, crying out in pain.

"Gahh!"

"Nathan!" Ylaine reached for him, but the tendrils of magic dragged him off the bank. The water churned into a froth around him, and when it cleared, Ylaine could only stare in horror as Nathan flailed below the surface, a newly-transformed Merman.

She gazed at Nayidia, who had changed, but the form was not unfamiliar. "You're the sea witch? The one who wanted to get revenge on my father?"

"Revenge?" Nayidia screeched. "No, you pathetic polyp, I wanted power! Davor was already bitter at the humans for the disappearance of his wife, it was too easy to make him think there was some way to overthrow the land-dwellers! And having that fat, lazy servant in my employ would take care of things on the surface—till you had to meddle in that, you insufferable eel!" She watched Nathan thrashing limply as he tried to manage a tail and gills all at once. "Good thing I can improvise."

"What will happen to him?" Ylaine's voice quivered as she asked.

Nayidia waved her hand, and the water around her swelled in preparation to carry her and Nathan away forever. "Oh don't worry; he'll get used to it. Enjoy the human life, Kelpling. I hope this little adventure taught you a lesson on what love really gets you! I guess you spoke too soon when you said he didn't love you, and now it's too la-*aaaiiieee!*" As she was speaking, Nathan burst out of the water and wrapped his scaly arms around her shoulders, dragging her backwards into the water. Nayidia twisted, but Nathan would not let go. "Get off me! " she shrieked, shoving madly at him. "What do you think you're doing?" Nathan had his hands around the witch's neck like he wanted to choke her, but she broke his grasp. Before she could grab him, Nathan raised his hand to throw something, crying, "Ylaine, catch!"

The object glinted in the sunlight, and Ylaine reached out just in time to snag something long and thin with her fingertips. A round gold object winked at her. The cowrie necklace!

Nayidia saw Ylaine fastening the chain around her neck and clutched at her own empty one. "You miserable prawn!" She snarled at Nathan, "That necklace is *mine!*" He tried to evade her, but she caught his neck in her long, bony fingers and began to squeeze. *"You are mine!"*

"STOP."

The command rang with a heavy knell, and Nayidia could not disobey. Her hands dropped, and Nathan sank to just below the surface, where he was safe.

"No, Nayidia," Ylaine continued, "It is you who spoke too soon, for I know that Nathan truly loves me: what better demonstration of true love can anyone give, than the willingness to give up one's life?" She solemnly drew her chin up as the golden glow of the sun broke through the trees. "Now I have reclaimed everything I forfeited, and the sun has not yet set." She pointed westward. "You can do nothing," she stated.

Nayidia tried to attack one last time, but Ylaine spoke truly. She could not so much as touch either

Ylaine or Nathan. Screeching horribly, the witch dove deep and swam out to the farthest reaches of the sea.

Ylaine dropped to her knees at the edge of the water. "Nathan!" She cried.

He could barely even pull himself up onto the bank just below her. His bulbous fish eyes swiveled to look at her, and she heard the same shallow, gasping breath she had felt when trying to breathe air with gills. He ducked his head to take water into his mouth. "This is a bit of a switch," he quipped.

Ylaine gave a little laugh in spite of the tears streaming down her face. She ran her hand through his hair as he laid his head on her knee. "There has to be something I can do!" She insisted—but what kind of magic did she have to change his form? She glanced at the small purse where she had tucked the remainder of the potion before her mad dash to the Carnival— "Oh wait," cried Ylaine, "the vial!" She quickly dug it out. A tiny sip of that glittering liquid sparkled in the bottom of the small bottle. Carefully, Ylaine removed the stopper and poured it into Nathan's mouth.

She had to grab his hand as his body curled up in pain, but she saw his tail separate, and the scales fade into human skin. In a few minutes, he raised his head and looked at her—

And Ylaine knew for certain that they both would remain human for the rest of their lives.

"Thank you, Ylaine," murmured Prince Nathan.

She clasped his hand in hers and kissed it. "I love you, Nathan," she whispered back.

"Your Majesties!" A familiar voice called out from beyond the sand dune.

"We are here, Giles!" Ylaine called.

Giles followed the voice till he found the pair—Ylaine, kneeling on the bank looking hale and hearty and yet completely spent, holding the hand of Prince Nathan, who clung to the rocky bank, half in the water and inexplicably naked. The steward stopped in his tracks.

"What happened?" He demanded.

Nathan and Ylaine shared a glance. "All in good time," said the Prince. "Meanwhile, might I borrow your cloak?"

He had no sooner finished asking than Giles was unfastening the garment in question. "Of course, my prince." He spread it so that Nathan could climb out of the water and spread the long woolen covering over himself.

"I take it your plan worked, Nathan?" Asked the servant wryly as they stood together.

Nathan grinned at Ylaine, who smiled shyly back. "Almost; there is still one question I want to ask you, Ylaine."

Her smile dimmed in confusion. "What is that?"

Nathan stopped, took both her hands in his and asked her, "Will you marry me, Princess Ylaine?"

Would she? Whatever feelings she had attributed to love before were all fickle and shallow in the light of how far he had proven willing to go for her sake. Would she entrust her life to a man who was ready at a moment's notice to give up his for her? "Yes, Nathan," she replied with a smile. Together they began walking down the path to return to the carnival.

"Very well," Giles nodded, "but there is still the matter of your guests from Crossway to attend to."

Nathan snorted. "You mean the fake queen and her daughter? Now that I have actually met the sea witch—"

Giles stopped in his tracks. "You what?"

Nathan huffed and brought the cloak closer around him. "Never mind; Giles, I would really appreciate some dry clothes."

The trio had reached a thicket on the edge of the carnival. Giles pointed to a tent right in front of them.

"You can no doubt find extra clothes in there. I will go in first to make sure it's clear."

"Perfect," answered Nathan. He turned to Ylaine. "You won't go far from this area without us?"

"Of course," she answered.

Moments after the prince and a steward ducked into the tent, Ylaine's quick ears caught the sound of uproarious laughter coming from nearby. Curiosity got the better of her, and she slipped out of the thicket to see what was going on.

A crowd had gathered not far from the spot where Devaine had turned the tables on her attempt to expose the false queen. Everyone was fixated on something happening in the area; not even the minstrels were playing anymore. Ylaine softly scooted around the crowd till she could see into the middle of it.

Devaine and Melinda huddled at the center. Their regal robes and flounces and jewels were gone, replaced by drab clothing in rough linen fabrics. People jeered at them—especially those they had sneered at.

"Not so high and mighty now, eh?"

"Fraud!"

"Faker!"

"You ought to be whipped for an impersonation like that!"

"Take them before the king!"

Ylaine gasped when someone grabbed her hand—but it was only Nathan.

"What is happening?" He whispered to her, craning his neck to see.

"I don't know," Ylaine whispered back, "but I fear something awful is going to happen to those ladies if we don't intervene."

Nathan was about to object to her sentiments when a voice called over the crowd, "What is the meaning of this?"

A tall, broad-shouldered nobleman stepped into the center of the crowd.

Devaine gasped, and she and her daughter cowered before him.

Nathan glanced at Giles and saw that his servant was grinning.

"Who is that?" Nathan hissed to him, but at that moment, Devaine seemed to answer his question.

"Lord Jamison," she gasped quaveringly, "I—I..."

Lord Jamison of Crossway folded his arms over his chest. "When Prince Nathan of Overcliff informed me by letter that my missing servants would be found this very night at this very carnival, I was hesitant to take him at his word."

Ylaine glanced at Nathan, who shrugged. They kept listening as Jamison continued.

"Then I hear tell of a pair of Royal visitors to the island kingdom when there had been no formal proclamation, and so I come to marvel at this wonder," he sneered at the women, "and what do I find? The same pair of servants missing from my employ, apparently here on a very deceptive holiday without my leave!"

Nathan began pushing his way through the crowd, pulling Ylaine with him.

"Lord Jamison!" He called. "Milord!"

Jamison turned to see who called him.

"And who might you be?" He demanded of the young man with a lady in tow.

"I am Prince Nathan," he explained.

Devaine and Melinda trembled in fear now; clearly they had expected Nayidia to get the better of the young couple.

Jamison's eyes widened. "Let me shake your hand, sir! I am indebted to you for exposing this most heinous charade!"

"Then these, indeed are the women you seek, Milord?" Asked Ylaine.

Lord Jamison shrugged. "They are, indeed! With your majesty's permission—" he glanced at the young prince, and Nathan nodded.

Jamison signaled two burly men carrying shackles. "Seize them!" He pointed to the women. Once the impostors had been carted away, the crowd dispersed back to their amusements. Jamison remained a moment to speak with Nathan.

"Your Highness, I apologize on behalf of the Royal Court of Crossway for any misdeeds these women have committed in the Royal name. If any recompense is needed—"

Nathan shook his head. "Nothing was done yet... But perhaps, in lieu of compensation, I may show you some ideas for reforming the economy of Overcliff; I am quite certain we would welcome any assistance

Crossway can offer in this matter."

"You have it, most assuredly!" Said Jamison. "Let us convene at a later time so that you can show me these plans of yours!"

Nathan nodded and began walking back toward the castle, but Ylaine slipped her hand out of his.

Nathan glanced at her with a questioning look in his eye, but she waved him on.

"Go back without me," she said. "I must speak with my father on several matters." She nodded back toward the path to the cove.

Nathan understood the reference. "Very well. Come up to the castle when you have finished."

Ylaine grinned. "Of course I will."

"I love you."

"I know," replied the princess, "and I love you, too."

The End

Leslie Conzatti is an avid writer and a voracious reader residing in the Pacific Northwest. Equipped with a vibrant, active imagination, Leslie has been crafting stories and creating fantasies out of the world around her and the one within her mind since before she could read. From the start of the very first book, Leslie has been committed to the production of lasting literature intended to invest in the lives of her readers, motivating them to become more involved in the world around them. Leslie holds a Bachelor's degree in English, and when she's not pegging away at the myriad story ideas she has started in her spare time, Leslie works as an elementary school staff assistant, teaching kids the intricacies of reading and writing English.

Further samples of Leslie's works, updates on current projects, and book reviews can be found on her blog: www.UpstreamWriter.blogspot.com

EndlessPress.org